"You're not the sort I usually run across."

Bourne bent and kissed her firmly but impersonally. "And you frighten the life out of me with your cast-iron armor. But you're not really unwilling, Lorena—admit it."

Shame washed over Lorena. "Stop it!" she managed to whisper at last. "I had no intention—"

"Oh, don't take me for a fool," he interrupted harshly. "You've had me wondering about your game ever since you got here. Advance, then retreat; and all the time that air of untouched sweetness. Just what do you want of me, Lorena Tanner?"

She swung herself off the chaise lounge, her expression as scornful as the sparkle in her golden eyes. "I don't want anything of you...."

"Anything but you" is closer, she thought—but swore she'd never let him know.

ROBYN DONALD
is also the author of these

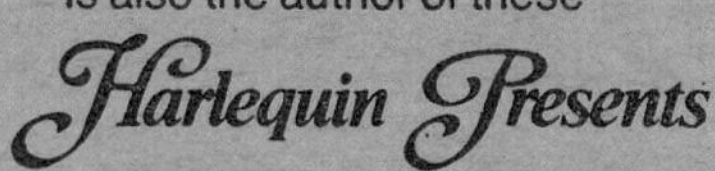

232—BRIDE AT WHANGATAPU
260—DILEMMA IN PARADISE
285—SUMMER AT AWAKOPU
303—WIFE IN EXCHANGE
320—SHADOW OF THE PAST

Bay of Stars

by

ROBYN DONALD

Harlequin Books

TORONTO • LONDON • LOS ANGELES • AMSTERDAM
SYDNEY • HAMBURG • PARIS • STOCKHOLM • ATHENS • TOKYO

Original hardcover edition published in 1980
by Mills & Boon Limited

ISBN 0-373-02391-X

Harlequin edition published March 1981

Printed in U.S.A.

CHAPTER ONE

THE large, unwieldy package she held couldn't disguise Lorena Tanner's grace as she manoeuvred it down the wharf. It was early in the season yet, barely December, so there weren't the crowds that high summer could bring, but the wharf at Paihia had its complement of tourists waiting for the ferry to take them across to historic Russell over the bay, and their glances were admiring.

One, a bearded figure with his country's maple leaf prominently displayed on his rucksack, asked in a pleasant Canadian accent, 'Hey, can I give you a hand with that?'

Lorena smiled, for his glance was frank and open, but shook her head. 'No, thanks, it's not heavy, and that's my transport down there.'

'Down there' was a runabout, small but luxuriously appointed, and an elderly man, thick and short, clad impeccably in white with a battered yachting cap pushed back to reveal a tanned bald head.

'Sel!'

His head jerked upwards at Lorena's cry. With a smile softening the craggy toughness of his features he swung up on to the pontoon and took the parcel from her.

'Still got that thing?' he asked, as if it had not been nine months since he had seen her.

Lorena grinned, her expression vivid and so alive that for a moment everyone else appeared pale and tired. 'Yes, and this time I can use it properly! I can hardly wait to get a good look at the stars without Auckland's lights getting in the way.'

'Funny way to spend your nights,' said Sel, but he looked as indulgent as it was possible for him to look. 'Hand me your bag and I'll put it below.'

'How's Peggy?'

'Fine.' He reappeared from the small cabin. 'She'll be glad to see you.'

'And I'll be glad to see her.'

A small boy threw the rope down into Lorena's hands. Smiling her thanks, she coiled it neatly as the outboard purred into life and the small boat swung away from the wharf. Then, leaning against the cabin, she drew in great drafts of the warm, salt-scented air, half-closing her eyes so that the sun made dazzling rainbows across her lashes. A contentment so strong that it was nearly ecstasy made her silent, almost drugged with happiness.

Born and brought up in the big, brash city of Auckland, she had fallen in love with this northern part of New Zealand on a trip made here when she was a child. Sun and sea and the long lazy days, the vivid colours and the dramatic seascapes had welded chains about her heart, so that when, years later and parentless, she had been looking for a job to tide her over the long summer vacation from university, she had applied for one on the southern shore of the lovely Bay. Peggy and Sel Robinson had come down to Auckland to interview her, and fortunately they had all taken a liking to each other, so the past three Christmases had been spent at Waiwhetu Bay. An appropriate name, she thought, for an amateur stargazer, as it meant 'the water which reflects stars', and on the still summer nights the bay was a sheet of obsidian transfixed with the wavering diamonds of the stars.

The deep note of a larger engine obtruded; Lorena opened her eyes and saw the turquoise and white ferry on its way to Paihia. An arm waved from the wheelhouse. She waved back, and several passengers replied, their smiling faces somehow symptomatic of the Bay's atmosphere.

'Oh, it's *good* to be back,' she exclaimed. 'Sel, who have we to look after this year? Not—not Mr Read?'

He grinned at that, for Mr Read, the owner of Waiwhetu Bay, was an American impresario of erratic habits, who had bought the place some ten years before and had never set foot in it since. He was, however, in the habit of lending the place to anybody he thought looked tired or jaded, and as his circle of friends and acquaintances was wide, there had been some strange guests at Waiwhetu. Last summer, for example, had been the year of a lady trapeze artiste who had lost her nerve, and a modern composer who was trying to write a symphony made up entirely of the sounds of breaking glass. They had taken an instant dislike to each other and the other two members of the party, so the entire summer had been spent trying to ensure that they avoided each other. A nerve-racking process, to say the least.

So it was with a keen interest that Lorena awaited Sel's answer. Nor was she disappointed when it came.

'Another composer, only this one I've heard of. Got his records, in fact. Bourne Kerwood.'

'*Really?*' She knew his records, of course, everyone did. Bourne Kerwood's smouldering dark gaze had been on too many record sleeves to miss notice. Lorena had once wondered if he was as impossibly good looking as he appeared. Now, it seemed, she was to find out. It would be exciting to meet a celebrity of this magnitude.

'Who is with him?' she asked.

'Nobody. He's trying to compose, apparently, and wants no one around. So there's to be no mention of his name. Peg told him that no one was likely to rush the gates—New Zealanders accept celebrities gracefully—but apparently he doesn't believe her. So—no name. He's got a passion for privacy.'

'You hardly need me, then,' said Lorena. 'I mean —one person! Peg could look after him with her hands tied behind her back.'

'Just you wait! She's got enough work lined up to keep you busy for months. We had the decorators in over the winter and she needs a hand setting the bedrooms to rights. And there's the bottling. The early plums are just about ready.'

Lorena heaved a heartfelt sigh at this, but smiled too. Peggy was justly famous for her preserving, and extremely fussy about it. Still, it was good training for the day when she would be in charge of a home, Lorena thought comfortably.

A seagull, hoping that they were fishing, wheeled overhead as the boat rounded Tapeka Point, dotted with its new houses above the beach. Out to sea the Ninepin rose tall and sheer; a little later in the season the big-game fishing launches would hunt around its wave-washed base. It was hot even for late spring, but the breeze whipped up by the boat's passage was sufficiently cool for Lorena to keep her jacket on.

'What's Mr Kerwood like?' she asked idly.

Sel shrugged. 'See for yourself. Better than last year's one by a mile, but that's not saying over much. We could put a line out and troll for Kahawai. Look, the birds are working.'

Lorena took the wheel while he got the gear ready, aiming into the heart of the cloud of terns, Kahawai birds, as they chased the sprats also pursued by the slender Kahawai, the freebooter of the sea. Three seasons of practice had given Lorena the confidence to cope with the boat, although at the beginning of each summer she was always worried in case a rock had sprung up over the winter in an unsuspected place.

It was the weekend, so the yachts were out, glorious things like multicoloured birds on the glittering, sparkling water. And there were other runabouts, some buzzing busily on their lawful business, others stationary as their occupants fished.

Twice they trolled through the turbulent water where the Kahawai fed, but nothing struck the spinner, so with a shrug Sel turned for home, threading his way through the islands which gave the lovely bay its name. Redcap, Motukete, Moturoa, there were myriads of them, the *Motu* prefix denoting an island. Some of them were tiny, others large enough to be farmed, but most had houses on them, a caretaker's cottage, the main house and often guest houses as well.

Mr Read had not fancied an island for his hideaway, so Waiwhetu Bay was chosen, and there he had built his house on the headland above the crystal waters and smooth pink melon slice of beach. From the sea it was almost impossible to see the house, so snuggled down it was amidst the pohutukawa trees, but Lorena always watched keenly as they came across the smooth waters of Parekura Bay.

Yes, there it was, dark-stained wood in the shade of the trees, the jetty thrusting out from the rusted red rocks of the headland. From the jetty a track, negotiable by four-wheeled drive, wound up to the house, but you couldn't see much of that from the sea either, and nothing at all of the footpath which descended the cliff to the beach.

There was land access to Waiwhetu Bay, but the road was narrow and dusty in summer, though every corner and hilly climb had its breathtaking views over the bay. Sel preferred to go by sea, and so, by and large, did the guests.

As the boat sped towards the jetty Lorena wondered just what Bourne Kerwood would be like. His records were superb, each an individual statement of one man's vision to which none of the popular labels could be applied. Like all artists he took his medium and created from it a personal ambience made up of his voice and his talent as a composer of both music and lyrics which were as haunting as any poetry Lorena had ever read. It was this intensely personal welding of melody, emotion and thought which gave him his immense popularity.

Probably, she thought, remembering dark intense good looks, he would be a conceited, arrogant, thoroughly unlikeable man, far too conscious of his talent and his wealth to be pleasant. Which would be a pity because she would never be able to hear one of his songs without remembering his less than likeable character. Still, it would be interesting to meet a super-star.

When the boat nosed into the jetty she sprang on to the sun-warmed planks with the rope in her hand, looped it around a bollard and took the parcels Sel handed up to her, groceries, her bag, and finally the awkward cardboard box which held the telescope.

'Seen anything good through that lately?' Sel asked.

'Oh, just a few stars. Auckland's lights make it hard.'

'You go on up,' he told her. 'I've got a few things to do here. Peg will have heard us come so she'll have the kettle on. Tell her I'll be up in twenty minutes or so.'

'O.K.' Happily she walked down the jetty, passed from the shimmering heat of the day into the dark coolness beneath trees which had clung to this headland for centuries. Much as Lorena liked Sel she would always have chosen to come to Waiwhetu like this, alone in the lateness of spring to wait in anticipation for the miracle which was almost here as silvery clusters of buds opened into tassels, crimson and scarlet, gold-tipped, so thickly joined that each sombre tree was transformed into a torch against the sky. It would happen again in a few weeks' time; indeed, on the Paihia waterfront one small tree bloomed bravely, confidently, lone harbinger of the year's glory.

On an impulse Lorena stretched, ran her fingers down the gnarled, rough bark of the nearest pohutukawa, her expression totally absorbed in the sensuous delight of being young and in tune with her world.

'Charming,' a cool masculine voice commented, the American accent investing the word with more warmth than the tone of voice implied. 'But you are trespassing, you know.'

At the sound of his voice Lorena had started almost guiltily, so perhaps he could be excused for jumping to conclusions. Turning to face him, she said as demurely as she could, 'I'm not—as it happens I work here.'

He had been standing in a patch of shadow so dense that she could make out only his outline. Now he stepped out into the lesser dimness, his dark brows drawn together over eyes which were every bit as mesmeric as they had appeared on millions of record covers.

Handsome as his most skilfully posed publicity photograph, he was well above middle height, clad in a pair of jeans and a cotton knit shirt which revealed at its open neck a thin gold chain with some sort of medallion on it.

In a voice cold with suspicion he demanded, 'You're the girl—the college kid?'

'I refuse to believe that Peggy called me that,' she said calmly. 'I'm Lorena Tanner.'

'You look far too beautiful to have brains too.'

For a moment she didn't believe that she had heard aright. Of all the chauvinists! With a slight shrug she remembered that she was an employee and he a guest of Mr Read's, and with a smile which she hoped was kindly but firm she replied, 'Stranger things have happened, Mr Kerwood.'

'Not many,' he returned. 'Where's Sel?'

'Down on the wharf.'

The nod he gave her was dismissal pure and simple. 'I'll see you around.'

That didn't need an answer, Lorena went her way without speaking, an uneasy sensation between her shoulder blades making her aware of the fact that he watched her until she was out of sight, the glory of the day dimmed by his rudeness.

Once up the hill she allowed herself a big shrug, her lips formed a soundless 'Phew!'

Too much, she told herself as she wended her way across the small patch of grass which was the only lawn. Just as well he seemed unpleasant or all that male charisma might turn her head. Not that he had shown the slightest interest in her as a person in spite of his comment about her prettiness. And why should he? Lorena knew very little about his life or background, but she had read enough of the antics of stars to know that beautiful women featured largely in their lives. There was no reason why Bourne Kerwood should be any different from the rest of them, if more discreet.

'Hi, King,' she said, stooping to pat the head of Peg's huge Alsatian dog. His lack of noise showed that he remembered her, recognising her as someone who had the right to be on the premises. Now he yawned, butted her hand with his head and allowed her to scratch him in that certain spot behind the ears, his tail swishing slowly from side to side.

As her fingers moved through his thick coat she looked around her with a pleasure made all the keener because of her absence. This patch of ground was Peggy's, a lovely border of flowers and shrubs around the handkerchief-sized lawn with its path leading out to the rotary clothes hoist in the centre. Behind were the huge old pohutukawas, beneath them a selection of shrubs chosen to endure conditions so close to the sea; sheltered by them were Peggy's plants, the bearded irises in full flower now, all shades from pure white through cream to blues so dark as to be almost black, pinks and lilacs and all sorts of bronzes. There were clumps of vividly coloured verbenas, herbs all fragrant in the salty air, spikes of gladioli and rose bushes blooming in their spring flush.

And over it all the sound of the bees as they plundered the blossoms against the soft stillness which the proximity of the sea gave Waiwhetu.

'Finished gloating?'

Lorena grinned affectionately at the tall plumpish woman who was regarding her with irony from the back doorway.

'Yes, I've finished for the time being; your garden looks lovely, Peggy.'

Peggy cast a not unsatisfied eye around her domain. 'It does look good this year. Come on in and I'll put the kettle on.'

'Sel said he'd be up in ten minutes.'

The house was big but not overwhelming, the rear portion so imbued with Peggy's personality that it seemed almost homely. As she followed her through the short passageway which led to the kitchen Lorena thought she would know a house of Peggy's anywhere. It would be extremely clean, very tidy and yet comfortable, with a special faint perfume of the lavender and beeswax mixture with which Peggy polished the furniture. There would be charming but informal bowls of flowers, a knitting bag by a rocking chair and a big fluffy grey cat in the same chair, a small colour television set with a lace doily on top of it and the crossword from the newspaper almost finished on the kitchen table. And never very far away the sound of a kettle, ready for the numerous cups of tea which both Sel and Peggy found necessary during the day.

'Meet Mr Kerwood on the way up?' asked Peggy.

'Yes. He told me I was trespassing.'

Peggy made her special noise, a cross between a grunt and a snort which could express very fine shades of emotion. 'He's got a passion for privacy, that one,' she commented. 'Makes you wonder what sort of life they lead over there. Hounded, by the sound of it.'

From which Lorena deduced that Peggy liked him. If she had taken one of her dislikes she would have made no effort to excuse what she saw as a foolish desire for privacy.

Somewhat surprised, for the very modern and extremely sensuous Bourne Kerwood shouldn't really appeal to someone as conventional as the housekeeper, Lorena ventured, 'How long is he going to stay?'

'Who knows?' Peggy set cups and saucers down on the table. 'He says he's getting ideas together for a record, but he seems to spend most of the time striding around the sitting room, glowering.'

Lorena could imagine that only too clearly. 'Perhaps that's how he composes,' she commented.

'Perhaps.' Peggy sent her a dry, direct glance. 'Do you find him interesting?'

'Reluctantly.' A mischievous smile touched the corners of her lips. 'Don't look so horrified. I knows me place.'

'I should hope so! He's trouble, that one. Far too much of what it takes to be interesting—too intelligent, too highly strung and bad-tempered to boot. A handsome bundle of dynamite.'

Lorena dropped into a chair, somewhat taken aback by the flat certainty of the older woman's tones. 'Yet you like him?'

'More trouble,' Peggy retorted. 'I doubt if many

could resist him. Things come easily to him, but there's a price to be paid, and he knows it. Pleasures jade swiftly when they're too easily won. He's finding that out now.'

'You seem to know him well. How long has he been here?'

'Long enough. He's not the sort to talk about himself, but I've seen a few like him in my life, and read of others.'

The warning was plain, and left Lorena a little shaken by Peggy's earnestness, the note of grimness in the housekeeper's pleasant light voice. There could be no doubt that the older woman meant every word she said.

'I suppose he's been spoilt by all of the adulation and praise,' Lorena responded after a moment. 'It would be almost inevitable, I'd imagine.'

'He was spoilt by Fortune,' Peggy stated crisply, producing one of her old-fashioned sayings which always fitted the context. 'Anyway, you'll see for yourself what he's like, although I doubt if he'll be around much longer. He doesn't seem to be getting anywhere and I'd say he's the restless sort.'

Sel came in then and the subject was dropped as they caught up with the nine months which had elapsed since they last saw each other. Peggy was no letter-writer, so they did not correspond, but both she and Sel enjoyed hearing of Lorena's year, and there was the gossip of the Bay for them to tell her.

At last Peggy put down her twice filled cup, saying reluctantly, 'Well, I suppose I'd better get dinner ready. Lorena, you go and get yourself unpacked. I'll not want you for anything tonight. Go and have a swim when you've got your room to rights.'

There were two bedrooms in the Robinsons' apartment at the back of the house, but Lorena's room was across a corridor and separate, a large bed-sitting room with its own miniscule bathroom and wide sliding glass doors on to a tiny terrace gay with pots of rose-red, pink and white pelargoniums. A step led down on to a patch of lawn and from there on to a path to what was known as 'the staff's beach', a tiny cove which was completely private.

There could be no doubt, Lorena thought, as she transferred her clothes into the immense empty wardrobe, that Mr Read's architect had the American's flair for making superbly comfortable homes. Her room was decorated in cool blues and greens and whites, with the airy lace-like patterns of cane furniture repeating the summery theme.

And the view! From her terrace she could look through the pohutukawa trees to the other side of Parekura Bay, the big area of water which held Waiwhetu Bay in its embrace. The water was vivid blue, gleaming and sparkling in the afternoon sun, the headlands green, with the occasional roof to show where houses were hidden and behind them, to the south, the high forest-covered hills of the coastal range.

The main part of the house looked north over the Bay of Islands proper, and that was beautiful too, but Lorena would not have traded it for her own personal glimpse of paradise.

As she breathed in the warm drowsy air, a tui called, a lovely cadence of notes like tiny gongs. Across the bay a small runabout left a wake like a water-beetle, a spreading fan of turbulence. A seagull wheeled, caught in the sun and became silver.

Lorena swallowed. Her eyes brimmed with tears

as that pain which is a necessary part of beauty held her in sweet sadness.

Then she turned and slipped back into the room, found her bathing suit and climbed into it. Mr Read—or his architect—had seen to it that there was a huge mirror on a wardrobe door, a mirror which showed a full-length Lorena without distortion. Once in her suit she stood looking at herself in it, wondering why Bourne Kerwood had called her beautiful.

She had a good figure, fashionably slender, with high breasts and a narrow waist, feminine hips and long legs kept supple by plenty of exercise. An impecunious university student walked wherever she could!

Yes, for the body, fairly high marks. But the face! High cheekbones, a square chin, a mouth which was firmly held beneath eyes of the strangest green-gold with flecks which one poetic boy-friend had sworn were purple! Above them narrow winged brows of dark brown and hair which was the chestnut of a well groomed horse, sleek and thick and short, for it was too unmanageable if allowed to grow.

Hardly beautiful, Lorena thought wryly; if one felt like being kind one could call it arresting, but far from the conventional ideals of beauty.

The irony of her actions made her turn swiftly from the mirror. How silly to inspect herself as if she could newly see just because Bourne Kerwood had paid her a compliment. They were not unknown, but delivered in that American drawl with the dark eyes fixed on her features his words seemed to have a quality which made them stick. Or perhaps it was the insult which went with them, the sting in the honey-bee, she thought frivolously, determined to think no more of the infinitely disturbing Mr Kerwood. She was no star-struck adolescent to fall in love with a handsome face and a voice which made a simple love song as sensual as a remark from Cleopatra!

As she wound down the cliff to the cove she pondered on the fact that his songs were earthy and direct, yet capable of subtleties of meaning and emotion which would make them much more lasting than ephemeral hit-parade material.

There she went, thinking about him again! It took an effort of will to dismiss the chauvinistic Mr Kerwood from her mind, but she managed it without too much difficulty, keenly aware as she always was of the beauties of nature.

This would be her first swim of the year and she was under no illusions about the temperature of the water. It would feel freezing, even though she knew that it reached its peak temperature midway through November. Somehow the sea was always frigid until December.

But the cove still basked in the late afternoon sun, and when she put a toe gingerly into the water it felt like silk against her skin, clear and limpid.

Casting her inhibitions to one side, she let out a wild yell and ran down into the sea's embrace, striking out with an easy crawl which took her smoothly through small waves.

Delicious though it was she felt no inclination to linger, but when she made for the shore again felt a shock of anger at the sight of Bourne Kerwood sitting on a rock above her clothes, tautly hunched on his heels as though ready at any moment to spring into action.

'This cove is for the staff,' she pointed out as soon as she came within hearing.

He grinned unrepentantly, so that she was aware of a flaring animal magnetism which demanded a response. Almost he won an indication of this from her, but her sense of the fitness of things prevented any spontaneity.

'I didn't see a sign,' he said provocatively.

Lorena pushed her fingers through her hair, moulding it in sleek wet lines against her head. 'Of course there's no sign, but it's always been accepted. Guests have Waiwhetu itself.'

'I prefer this.' He stood up with one swift movement, displaying great strength and excellent balance. 'You can use Waiwhetu while I'm here.' He pronounced the unfamiliar Maori word as if he were a New Zealander.

Glancing away, Lorena shrugged, dropped her towel around her and said coolly, 'Very well, then, Mr Kerwood. If that's what you want.'

'It is.' His voice hardened. He came down from the rock with lithe grace and went on, still in that cold voice, 'Why are you up here?'

'Because I'm hired by Mrs Robinson,' she retorted with a snap.

'Do you think you're necessary?'

Lorena felt anger and doubt, and then more anger which swamped the doubt. 'That's for Mrs Robinson to decide,' she answered, setting off across the pink beach with firm determined steps.

Any hope that he might be content with undisputed possession of the cove died as she heard him come up behind her.

'No doubt it's easier for her to have you around,' he said with smooth directness, 'but I doubt if

Aaron Read would be happy to know that his money is being wasted.'

Lorena whirled to face him, her incredulous gaze fixed on the dark enigma of his face.

'And I suppose you'll make sure he hears,' she snapped trenchantly, anger touching her cheeks with fire.

'So you admit it's a put-up job?'

'No.' Holding tight control over her temper, she said crisply, 'Look, why don't you talk to Mrs Robinson? She hired me.'

'I'll do that. In the meantime, you're not to mention to anyone that I'm here.'

She could not resist the temptation. Allowing a gleam of contemptuous mockery to appear in the cool depths of her eyes, she said with more than a hint of superiority in her tone, 'You really needn't worry, Mr Kerwood. New Zealanders, by and large, are a well-behaved species and when a visiting celebrity—however famous—makes it obvious that he wants privacy we're inclined to grant it. I'm sure you won't be inundated by slavering teeny-boppers.'

That her taunt had hit home was easy enough to see. A flush of colour touched the bronzed skin across the high cheekbones and the glance became fixed, frighteningly intense.

Lorena took an involuntary step backwards, cursing herself for her too-ready tongue which had led her into this situation. Useless to remind herself that if he cared to he might well be able to get her the sack—and not only her, either, for the Robinsons had been included in that threat. He looked like an animal about to spring; without being too fanciful Lorena was reminded of the remorseless patience of a leopard she had seen on a television documentary and the blaze that had irradiated its eyes before it finally delivered the *coup de grâce* to its prey.

Considerably shaken by his reaction, she opened her lips to apologise, although it went sorely against the grain.

Forestalling her, he asked calmly, 'Do you always react so sharply to people you dislike?'

Colour washed over her face, making her seem much younger than her nineteen years. Without taking time to think she answered, 'No, but I lost my temper, which I know I should *not* do! At least—I don't dislike you. I don't know you.'

'I've hardly given you a chance to like me,' he said, that frightening anger suddenly replaced by amusement which rendered his attraction about a hundred times more potent. 'Come, let's shake hands and be friends.'

It seemed churlish to refuse, so she took the hand he extended, feeling an odd sensation as it closed around hers. It wasn't hard to return the smile he gave her; she had to believe that when Bourne Kerwood smiled few people resisted its charm, but she did say weakly:

'Hardly friends. I work here.'

'Oh?' He lifted his brows. 'I thought New Zealand was like the States only more so, definitely egalitarian. Isn't your attitude Victorian, to say the least of it?'

A little tug repossessed Lorena of her hand, but he took her elbow and turned her towards the path.

Still flustered by his abrupt change of mood, Lorena retained enough self-possession to say, 'Perhaps it is, but it's the easiest way to cope.'

'I refuse to believe that.'

Fortunately the path was too narrow for two to walk abreast, so he was forced to let her go. Relieved, she ran lightly up the cliff before him, almost as if she hoped that she would leave him behind.

He was, however, only one step behind her and not an atom out of breath when they finally reached the top.

Once there she turned and said definitely, 'It is, though.'

Laughing softly, he returned, 'Stop looking so determined, honey. You can try to keep the distinction between upstairs and below stairs as rigid as you like, but I refuse to be intimidated by a scrap of a girl barely out of the cradle. How old are you, seventeen? eighteen?'

'I'm nineteen,' she said shortly, resisting with every atom of her being his blatant charm. 'I'll have to go now, Mr Kerwood. I'm getting cold.'

And indeed she could feel the tell-tale shudder of her lower lip.

'O.K.,' he said lazily. 'I'll see you around, Miss Tanner.'

Which left her wondering just where that left things!

As she showered and rubbed her hair dry Lorena wondered about the man, why he had changed from being merely threatening to an anger so strong that it had really frightened her and then, as she watched, replaced that with genuine amusement. And why had he taken such an instant dislike to her? She could come to no conclusions about his behaviour, but some hitherto dormant instinct told her that he was a dangerous man. For her own peace of mind it might be well to stay well out of sight while he was around.

*

'He's not fussy about his food, but he likes it to be cooked properly and served nicely,' Peggy said, a trifle caustically. 'Eats a lot of fruit.'

'I thought Americans were great steak men,' Lorena commented with an idle lack of interest, setting the forks on to the red and white checked tablecloth.

'Maybe. This one hasn't turned a steak down, but he told me no huge portions of meat. Hop out and get me some basil and some chives, will you? Oh, and parsley.'

The herbs were honoured and important plants in the border. Lorena picked the triangular-leaved basil, sniffed appreciatively at the fragrant sprig and smiled as her eyes were caught by the brilliant blue star flowers of borage, mints all neatly confined in barrels by the hose tap and the clumps of garlic and chives tucked in between more conventional irises and pinks, snapdragons and marigolds. Like her domain in the house, Peggy's garden was an expression of her personality.

'Chop them into the tomatoes, will you?' Peggy asked when she arrived back into the kitchen.

It was pleasant to chop the herbs into the salad of tomatoes and spring onions, pleasant to make a dressing of lemon juice and olive oil and toss the salad until it gleamed, a symphony of red and green and white. Lorena hummed a song as she worked, then realised that it was one of Bourne Kerwood's hits and changed swiftly to a folk song, feeling oddly selfconscious, as though she had been caught out at something.

Apparently he ate later than the Robinsons, for Peggy dished up for the three of them first.

'You must be the best cook I know,' Lorena told

her appreciatively as she surveyed iced cucumber soup, cooling and beautiful.

'Not much of a compliment.' Peggy looked pleased, however. 'I don't suppose you know anyone who can cook properly.'

'I'm not too bad—thanks to you. But you're right. Our food doesn't exactly aspire to Cordon Bleu standards—too expensive.' Lorena grinned cheerfully, her wide mouth relaxing into mischief. 'I have to watch my pennies, you know. The bursary doesn't permit any luxuries, and although the lawyers are very good at advancing me any shortfall from the parents' estate, they're very sticky about dipping into capital. Not that there's much of that, either. The parents, bless them, were joyously impecunious types.'

When she had first come up to Waiwhetu Bay the loss had been too recent for her to discuss her parents, and Peggy and Sel had never broached the subject. Like all losses, however, the pain had grown less over the years, so that she was able to speak of them without the tremble in her voice which had afflicted her for so many years.

Peggy had her share of curiosity. However, she waited until the meal was finished and coffee was on the table before asking slowly, 'What did your father do? You said once that he was an artist of sorts.'

'He was an architect.' Lorena set her cup down, gazing out of the window at a pink cloud of flowers on a manuka bush, 'A very good one. He died in a diving accident when I was twelve. And then Mum's Parkinson's disease just galloped her away too. She died halfway through my first year at 'varsity. Perhaps she just didn't want to live without him.'

'Sad,' Peggy murmured, refilling Sel's tea-cup without being asked.

When it came to domestic matters these two operated on a sort of radar system, Lorena thought, and wondered rather forlornly if she would ever be so close to a man that she would be able to foresee his needs without a word between them.

Marriage seemed an odd institution, one that constricted while it provided security, of a sort. The alternatives didn't seem to have much going for them either. Lorena had noticed that those who lived together seemed to have the constrictions without the security, and those who lived alone paid for their freedom with periods of loneliness and boredom. So all in all it seemed as though marriage was the best bet for happiness, provided one chose one's partner carefully, which Lorena had every intention of doing.

'And how do you think your exams went?'

Lorena shrugged, answering honestly, 'If I don't get them I'll be furious with myself.'

Sel grinned. 'Fair enough. You're like him'—with a jerk of his head towards the front of the house—'no false modesty. Told me that his songs were popular because they had a beat, a good tune and said something.'

'He seems to have got himself a bit stuck for something to say this time around,' Peggy observed. 'He doesn't seem to have produced anything.'

'Been comparing his techniques with that twit we had last year?' Sel asked. 'The one who wanted to smash glass all over the place?'

Peggy snorted. 'There's no comparison to be

made. Mr Kerwood can sing, and he's quite right, his songs do say something. The other was a pretentious idiot.'

Which disposed of the subject and the meal, for she rose as she spoke, glancing at the clock over the table. 'Time to put his dinner out.'

CHAPTER TWO

THE next day saw the start of Lorena's job. It began with a knock at the back door and the delivery of four succulent flounder by the seventeen-year-old son of the farmer along the road.

'Hey!' he exclaimed when Lorena opened the door. 'You *are* here! How's things?'

She smiled, 'Fine. Are these for us?'

'Yeah. Got them last night, along with a ton of others, so Mum said to bring them along. Lorena, did you bring your 'scope?'

'Yes, I did.' She took the flounder and went on, 'Thank you very much for these, Gordon. Shall I give you a ring one night when conditions are good for viewing?'

'Do that. I've got a cousin up—Mark. He's a bit older than me. Can I bring him too?'

'Yes, of course. I'll have to go now, Gordon. Thanks a million.'

'He's back, is he?' Peggy seemed to find Gordon's arrival amusing. 'Thought he'd be along before long. I'll give Mrs Haworth a ring later and thank her for the flounder. We'll have them for lunch.'

To Lorena's astonishment Bourne Kerwood came into the room, almost revoltingly fresh-looking, clad in his favourite jeans and another shirt, pale cream this time, which threw his dark good looks into startling relief.

'Hi, Peggy,' he greeted her with lazy good humour. 'Hi, Lorena. Where's Sel?'

'Out vacuuming the pool.'

'Mm. Do you think he'd trust me with his runabout? I want to visit the island I can see from my bedroom window.'

'Bounderman's?' Peggy gave Sel's porridge a last stir, then nodded at the door. 'I'm sure he'll take you there. Ask him yourself.'

But he didn't want to be taken, as he pointed out to Sel with a thread of steel in the deep slow voice. 'I'm used to runabouts,' he said, when it was obvious that Sel wasn't convinced.

The two men faced each other. Lorena, feeling an odd compulsion to hold her breath, waited for Sel's capitulation. It didn't come. The older man surveyed the younger for a long moment, and then, as though receiving some sort of signal from his subconscious, relaxed and nodded.

'Very well, then,' was all that he said, but it released Lorena from that sudden tension.

'Good. I'll leave after breakfast.' Bourne turned, asking Peggy, 'Do you mind if I have it with you? It will save someone carrying it out. And will it be too much of a bind to pack me a lunch?'

He didn't pour on the charm, Lorena thought dispassionately, it was just there whether he wanted to use it or not. But not just charm. He possessed a kind of chemistry which was as potent as a witch's brew, a sensuality which probably reached out across the footlights to make every woman in every audience acutely conscious of her femininity. It came through on his records, too.

None of which explained why Sel, normally extremely jealous of his employer's possessions, had agreed to let him take the runabout. Sel would never say, but Lorena realised that for all of his appeal to the opposite sex Bourne Kerwood demanded and won respect from men. Which made him rather exceptional.

But then anyone who had got as far as he had must be exceptional, so why feel so surprised?

A question she didn't pursue, especially as she felt his glance on her and found herself wishing rather ardently that he didn't have quite such an effect on the opposite sex. Surely it was unfair to give a man almost everything in this life!

Rather pink about the cheeks, she went on setting the table.

It could have been an uncomfortable meal, but thanks to the Robinsons' self-confidence and the Kerwood *savoir faire* it passed by smoothly enough. Sel and he discussed fishing and various local doings in which he seemed to be really interested, to Lorena's further surprise.

Perhaps she revealed this, for he smiled somewhat mockingly across the table at her and said, 'I'm a small town boy myself. It's you city slickers who find life in the country dull.'

'Not me,' she defended herself crisply. 'I love Waiwhetu.'

'Ever been here in the winter?'

She smiled at his scepticism. 'Yes. I spent the August holidays here a year ago.'

'Enjoy it?'

'Well, it didn't rain all that much, but it was cold. Still I did enjoy it.'

Peggy said dryly, 'Only because you got a different lot of stars to peer at.'

'Stars?'

There was no mistaking the interest in the deep tones.

Shrugging slightly, Lorena told him, 'I'm a very amateur stargazer,' and wondered why she felt cross with Peggy.

'What do you use, binoculars?'

'No, I haven't got a pair. I have my father's old astronomical telescope.'

Somehow Lorena didn't want to talk about her love affair with the night sky even though he was so clearly interested, but the good manners her mother had inculcated forbade her to show any signs of her reluctance.

'And this of course would be a good place to look. The skies are almost as clear as those in the desert at home. Do you chase asteroids or search for comets in the hopes of discovering a new one?'

With another lift of her shoulders Lorena answered dryly, 'I content myself with discovering which stars are which, and peering at the planets.'

'Fair enough.'

And that was the end of the discussion. As if regretting the fact that he had allowed his animosity to be overshadowed by his interest he switched his attention to Sel, and for the rest of the meal did not address another remark towards Lorena, though she found the enigmatic darkness of his glance on her once or twice.

Unpleasantly surprised by the effect he had on her, she decided over the breakfast dishes that the less she saw of him the better. So Peggy's decision to tackle the newly decorated bedrooms was a welcome one, for in the hustle that followed she forgot completely about Bourne Kerwood.

Peggy didn't believe in keeping rigid hours of work, which meant that although Lorena was called on during the weekend she had more spare time each day than she would have otherwise. And as Peggy and Sel had reached the age when the hour after lunch, the hottest period of the day, was devoted to reading and resting on their cool, screened terrace, that meant that Lorena, perforce, had that hour to herself.

But she was too young and vital, too eager to grasp every hour of life, to want to waste it in resting. Clad in shorts and a brief cotton top, she decided to devote it to exploration, the renewal of her acquaintance with Waiwhetu Bay. As the one pampered guest was over on Bounderman's Island she felt no restraint about going down to the circle of beach backed by a hillside where native trees held their rounded canopies above undergrowth too dense to move through easily. Waiwhetu peninsula had never had livestock through it, so that it was almost in its primeval state. Lorena liked to pretend that she was the first person ever to find her way through the bush down on to the sand, cool under the spreading pohutukawa trees, but stingingly hot where the sun beat down upon it.

Mr Read—or his architect—had shown good taste here, too. The cabana was a small, darkly varnished building at one end of the beach, which blended perfectly into the background of trees and hillside.

Feeling like a Maori girl in the days when New Zealand was young and innocent, Lorena walked the full length of the beach towards the building, her feet making soft sounds on the cool wet sand. Once she let a wave catch her, but here in these sheltered waters the sea moved in a lazy motion, creaming to silence on the sand before slipping a little way back before repeating the process. A tame sea, Lorena thought, remembering the surf of the west coast beaches out of Auckland, with their euphonious Maori names, Piha, Muriwai. They had danger, those surf beaches, holes and rips, and you swam within the flags or took your life in your hands.

Waiwhetu was as safe as any beach could be, but even here, the sea was not to be trifled with. Cramp could strike beneath a sky as blue and serene as this one, and for those who swam alone that was as much a danger as being caught in a merciless Piha rip.

However, this did not deter Lorena from making use of Bourne Kerwood's permission to use Waiwhetu instead of the little cove across the headland. Sensibly she didn't over-exert herself, content to stroke up and down the beach a couple of times before drying off on the sand in the full rays of the sun.

Mindful of her skin, she stayed exposed to them for no more than the ten minutes it took to dry her bikini, then set off towards the cabana, her gaily coloured beach towel slung over one shoulder.

Just when she noticed the music she couldn't quite determine, for she was absorbed in the sheer physical pleasure of her surroundings, soaking in the warmth and stillness, the fresh moist smell of the bush and the tang of the sea, the sounds of sea-birds and the soft lapping of the waves.

Half drugged by it all, she was almost up to the beach house before she realised that what she was hearing was Bourne Kerwood singing to guitar accompaniment. Guiltily, like a trespasser, Lorena stopped, and impelled by a sense of self-preservation so strong that it was almost a terror, she swung under the overhanging branch of pohutukawa. A long moment she stood, listening with ears which disregarded any other sounds. Yes, it was he, singing a song she hadn't heard before. Without the orchestral backing he usually used it sounded completely different from his other songs, but there was no doubt that it was his composition, for it had that haunting combination of passion and melancholy which stamped his most popular compositions.

As if in danger of being caught eavesdropping, she began to slip back as quietly as she could under the sheltering arms of the pohutukawas. But her footsteps gave her away, for they marched triumphantly, openly, defiantly across the sand. And why should she feel like a thief in the night? He had told her to swim on Waiwhetu, and anyway, he was supposed to be zapping around Bounderman's or on the runabout, not singing in the beach cabin. It was stupid to feel so guilty.

So she strode forcefully back down the beach, angry with herself for being so frightened of him, angrier with him for spoiling her lovely freedom with his presence.

Whether he saw her she didn't know, but about half way down the beach her shoulder blades tautened as though somebody was willing her to turn around.

Stubbornly she held on to her course. He couldn't miss the footsteps, of course, but at least she wouldn't try to hide from him. She was, she told herself, an independent, thoroughly self-reliant woman, and no one, not even a super-star like Bourne Kerwood—if that was his real name and not a made-up one—could take that away from her.

Which made it all the more surprising that she discovered in herself a strong desire not to see him again that day, and an ominous sinking feeling in the region of her stomach whenever she thought of his likely comments about her intrusion. It made her inordinately thankful when Peggy decided to take his dinner in herself.

However, Peggy decided that Lorena should clear up.

Summoning up a large dose of stiffening in her backbone, she went through the house to the table under the pergola where he habitually ate.

Her hope that he would have gone died immediately, for he was leaning back in his chair, glowering at a cup of coffee as if he hated the stuff. At her approach, his glance lifted, became sharp and narrowed as the smile he bestowed on her.

'The fair eavesdropper,' he said softly.

Defensively she answered, 'You should post a 'DO NOT DISTURB' notice. In future I'll swim away from the cove.'

'Not necessary.' He grinned, drained his cup with a gesture and set it down, still smiling as if her defensiveness amused him. 'As it happens, you gave me an idea. It may not come to anything, but so far it's shaping up nicely.'

Sourly wondering if this was a favourite ploy of his, Lorena contented herself by raising an eyebrow as she stacked the dishes, her movements quick and deft across the table top.

'Don't you believe me?' he asked, still amused.

Lorena knew she was behaving badly, especially as this Bourne Kerwood was infinitely more pleasant than any previous guest, but she could not help feeling that he was having some obscure joke with her. Forcing herself to be polite, she answered, 'If you say so, I must, I suppose, but it seems most unlikely.'

'Fishing for compliments?'

Scarlet under his blatant, slow assessment of her face and body, she snapped, 'No, I don't need casual compliments, thank you.'

'Well, you certainly sound as if you don't get any, if that's your normal reaction to an appreciative stare.'

'That was a *leer*!'

He laughed, catching her hand as she moved away. 'Sit down and tell me all about yourself. And that's an order!' as she directed an angry frown down at him.

'What on earth can you want to know about me?' she asked, astonished into submission.

'Oh, everything. Come on—sit down. First of all,' as she obediently lowered herself into the chair opposite him, 'and try not to glare so suspiciously at me—are you really nineteen?'

'Yes.'

'Good God!' Dark brows lifted in surprise. 'You look about sixteen, a very knowing sixteen. You know, ever since I saw you I've been trying to work out where I'd seen you before, and it's finally come to me. Ever seen a photograph of the fantastic jewellery found at Ur by Leonard Woolley?'

'Ur of the Chaldees? In the Middle East?' Against her will he had caught her interest.

'Uh-huh. That Mr Woolley excavated the grave of a king and queen, and Mrs Woolley modelled wax over a skull to get some idea of how they looked. Like you, as it happens. The same cheekbones and firm jawline.' He grinned. 'So you see, you come from a long line—about five thousand years of beauty. I wonder if you could trace your ancestry back to Ur.'

The idea fascinated her, but she was not going to lose her head over a neat and novel line in compliments, so she said sedately, 'Are you interested in archaeology, Mr Kerwood?'

'Call me Bourne, for heaven's sake,' he directed with a note of impatience. 'Yes. I was going to be an archaeologist, but my music got in the way.'

Lorena permitted herself a smile as she rose. 'I don't think you would have made nearly such a big impression as an archaeologist,' she murmured as she grabbed the tray and made good her escape.

And let him make what he wanted to of that! she thought crossly. Then found herself wondering what that long-ago girl from the mists of time had looked like.

Peggy's swift glance seemed to stab. 'Did he want to talk?' she asked.

Lorena shrugged. 'Yes. He must be getting bored; I suppose he's used to having hordes of hangers-on around him all the time.'

'You don't like him?'

Cornered, Lorena frowned. 'No—it's not that really.' She could not, of course, tell Peggy that she was rather afraid that if she relaxed her guard at all she might find herself liking him too much. So she continued, 'He seems arrogant—spoiled, I suppose.'

'Natural enough.' Peggy shook the soap dispenser under the hot tap, watching the froth and bubbles with a dispassionate eye. 'Nobody can ever be brought up to cope with a life like his, unless it's the Royal Family. To be always in the limelight like that must be very tough on the character. If what you read about the stresses and strains and the power of these pop stars is true, he's come through it fairly well. That might be because he's made such a thing of his privacy.'

Lorena laughed as she removed the tea towel from the rack. There was a dishwasher under the bench, but Peggy preferred not to use it except in summer when water was scarce.

'It sounds,' Lorena teased, 'as though he's won your impressionable heart, Mrs Robinson.'

'Well, I'd hate any child of mine to live that sort of life,' Peggy defended herself. 'Apart from the temptations, it's an unnatural existence. No human being is equipped to deal with such adulation.'

'Oh, he seems well-balanced,' Lorena commented with airy smoothness. 'And I'll bet he's tough enough to cope with anybody or anything he's met up with. Behind the charming façade he's steel all through.'

'How do you know?'

Lorena felt a little puzzled at her certainty, but tossed off Peggy's curiosity by an assumed air of mystery. 'It's my instinct,' she said solemnly, pitching her voice low. 'And my instinct never lies! So be warned.'

'You're as mad as you ever were,' Peggy smiled. 'I'd have thought that two years at 'varsity would have sobered you up.'

'Oh, I'm a hopeless case. Frivolous as a butterfly, I'm afraid.'

And the awkward moment passed in their mutual understanding.

But much later that night, as she stood on her little terrace and watched the moon come up over the headlands past the tiny settlement of Rawhiti, Lorena wondered why she should be so confident of Bourne Kerwood's toughness. Reluctantly she was forced to own that perhaps instinct wasn't such a bad word for it; it was strange how some hidden part of her seemed to fix on the essential part of others. It had taken barely a minute or so for her to realise that Peggy and Sel were absolutely rock-steady reliability through and through. And she had always known the weaknesses which had eventually weaned her away from her various boy-friends; Peter who was a darling but too dependent; Roger who hid his inferiority complex with a hearty manner; even Garth, who tried desperately to be modern, but who was a firm believer in a woman's place being in the kitchen. And Mark, who possessed a cruelty which his sophistication had hidden by a mask of mockery.

Lorena shivered, turning away from the view. Mark had been hard to get rid of, the most persistent of all her suitors, and the one she liked least. It had been difficult to cope with his insistence that she marry him, even harder to cope with his disbelief and anger when he realised that he was not able to change her mind.

Well, that was all over now. When she had last heard of him, some three months ago, he had been almost engaged to someone else. Lorena hoped for their happiness, hoped very fervently that the girl knew what sort of man he was.

At least, she thought, smiling with self-mockery, at least Bourne Kerwood was not cruel—or not with Mark's calculation. He might be as hard as nails, but any cruelty would come from a loss of temper and probably regretted as soon as it occurred.

But she still felt that strong warning from whatever part of her worried over such things. He was a dangerous man to be around, especially when he showed himself in a pleasant mood as he had tonight. A star like Bourne Kerwood could find nothing interesting in a nineteen-year-old from New Zealand, who had no more than a moderate amount of good looks, a moderate amount of brains, and an equally moderate quantity of character. In his life he would have met the most beautiful and alluring women in the world, many of them, from what one read, only too keen to make themselves available in every way.

So—drawbridges up! Aloofness, she decided, would be her watchword, and if it irritated him, too bad! She didn't think that she was any more susceptible to men than most other girls, but it would be easy enough to fall hard for Bourne Kerwood and be left weeping!

With this determination firmly in her mind it was too bad that she should hear that slow drawl from the edge of the shrubbery.

'Where's your telescope, Copernicus?'

After the first shock of fear she felt a strange excitement race through her nerves. 'It's not a good night for viewing,' she returned, stifling her racing heart. 'The moon is too bright.'

Thank heavens she had come out clad in respectable jeans!

He moved up to stand on the grass just below the flower-hung edge of the terrace. In the moonlight he looked big and tough and exciting.

'I'd have thought that a full moon was ideal.'

'No. Ideally it should be two-thirds out to get the best view. You can see quite a bit if you look at it when it's full, but the shadows show up better before or after the full.'

'Can you see much now? At this moment, as it's

rising? It looks as if it's magnified for you.'

'Not really; it's too distorted by the atmosphere. Later on, when it's higher in the sky, is the best time to look.'

There was a flash of white as he smiled. 'I'll believe you,' he said cryptically. 'Care to come for a walk?'

Lorena would like to—but sanity prevailed. There was a lazy, knowing note in his voice which warned her that he saw her as a pretty girl, to be kissed perhaps under the moon. And she did not want his light, meaningless lovemaking.

So she returned, 'No, thanks.' And realising how curt that sounded, added lamely, 'At least, I'd like to, but I have work to do tomorrow.'

'Scared?'

She laughed, quelling the indignant refusal which he would not have believed. 'Terrified, Mr Kerwood. Have a pleasant walk. Don't let Rona take you unawares.'

'Rona?'

'The lady who lives in the moon. That's her you can see now with her gourd.'

'Hey, tell me about her!'

Lorena realised that he was really interested. Perhaps she had intended to hook his interest, for she made no demur about telling the age-old story of Rona, who had gone to fetch water in the dark, stumbled when the moon went behind a cloud and cursed it with the most potent curse she could think of. Instantly she had been snatched up into the moon and there you could see her today, with her empty gourd.

'That's great,' he said when she finished. 'How come you know a Maori legend?'

'Grew up on them; most New Zealanders have,' she answered flippantly, trying to break the mood which enveloped them, a mood of far too intimate a character.

'You've got something here, I hope you realise. No hatred, no history of oppression like we bear as a burden.'

'Oh, there was oppression, and there's some hatred—dislike, I suppose is a better word. New Zealand is not paradise, but it's a pretty good substitute, we think.'

'I'll go along with that.' He turned, then looked back over his shoulder, asking softly, 'Still determined to go to bed?'

'Very much so.'

He laughed, as if he didn't believe her, and strode off into the darkness cast by the canopy of a silk tree, leaving her more shaken than she cared to admit.

The next morning there was a scribbled note on the kitchen table—'Let me sleep!'

'Spent most of the night up,' Sel commented dryly. 'I heard him come back about four this morning. What's the P.S., Peggy?'

'He wants a book of Maori legends,' his wife told him without any surprise. 'You'd better get one from the bookshop in Paihia when you go across this morning.'

After breakfast it was time to 'do' the living areas of the house, the big sitting room, the games room with its billiard table and the smaller less formal garden room which was the favourite of most women, then the huge dining room which was so rarely used.

Lorena enjoyed her work, taking real pleasure

in the beautiful things which had been chosen so carefully to give comfort and pleasure.

After she had vacuumed the floor she dusted and polished, wondering as she always did, just where the dust came from in this place so far from the road!

Outside the sun's heat and light intensified, really summery now. The swimming pool glittered and sparkled, heightening the vividness of the flowers which surrounded it, so that it was a pleasure to lift her eyes to the cool shade of the trees. From across the bay somewhere came the sound of an inboard engine, thudding quietly through the stillness of the morning. Bees hummed and buzzed and danced their complicated dances, golden in the sun as they reaped toll from the flowers. Later on, when the pohutukawas were covered in their scarlet and crimson robes, the bees would concentrate on them and produce the famous honey which was accounted a great delicacy, but for the moment they were content with the blooms in the garden beds.

Lorena felt an uplift of her spirits which was the direct result of such a perfect day. Humming softly, she tidied the rooms, then brought in flowers and arranged them to their best advantage, complementing the cool green, white and gold colour schemes with touches of clear orange and apricot, lemon and the darker green of foliage.

The house really was beautiful; it seemed a crying shame that only guests enjoyed its mellow loveliness, she thought wistfully. It needed a family to cherish it before it revealed its full charm. Unfortunately that was never likely to eventuate.

'Envious, Lorena?'

The mocking enquiry from somewhere behind her brought an angry colour to her cheeks.

'Not in the least,' she retorted, turning to face him with her head held high. The colour in her cheeks deepened, for he was clad only in swim shorts and even across a room he had altogether too powerful an effect on her senses.

'You must have seen a man like this before,' he taunted, those dark eyes fixed on her face, making it quite clear that her embarrassment amused him.

'Of course I have,' she said stiffly. 'I'll go and tell Peggy you're up so she can get your breakfast ready.'

'Sure, you do that,' he drawled. 'I'll have it in half an hour.'

Lorena made good her escape, feeling as gauche as the most self-conscious fifteen-year-old, and scolded herself all the way into the kitchen. Just because he looked like the archetypal male there was no reason to lose her self-possession so spectacularly. So—he had a considerable effect on her! So what? she demanded of herself. It was a purely physical thing, a kind of masculine version of allure, and Bourne Kerwood had enough of it to share, or he probably wouldn't be such a famous singer.

After all, a man who could project his brand of sensuality was bound to be a hit with at least fifty per cent of his audience. But even as she told herself this she knew that she was wrong. When he sang it was the songs, the power and beauty inherent in them, which caught the heart and remained in the memory.

Unfortunately she would remember him for his disturbing masculinity!

'Take his breakfast in, there's a good girl,' said Peggy when she'd received the message. 'You know where he eats. Grapefruit juice, cereal, and those stewed tamarillos. He likes them.'

'Who wouldn't?' Lorena looked down at the dark crimson fruit and juice. 'I like them best with ice-cream, though. Or in your upside-down cake.'

'Well, *he* likes them with his cereal. Get a move on, girl, or he'll be shouting for his food.'

'He's swimming,' said Lorena, but subduing her desire to suggest that Peggy take the tray through, she began to put the wherewithal on to it with competent briskness.

He was still swimming when she arrived at the white table beneath the pergola, slicing through the water with the ease and smoothness of much practice, tanned arms hauling his body the length of the pool.

Lorena set the table and disappeared as quickly as she could.

CHAPTER THREE

THE days settled down into a routine, made easier by the fact that Bourne spent much of his time in the beach cabana, appearing at odd hours for breakfast and then disappearing again. Presumably composing, or so Peggy and Sel decided. He wasn't thoughtless about meals, apologising charmingly when he was late, but he worried Peg, who was sure that he wasn't getting enough to eat, and who took to sending Sel down to fill up the refrigerator in the cabana with snacks, containers of various salads, and an assortment of rolls and cheese.

'He won't starve,' she said, 'but he should be eating regularly, not snatching snacks at all hours of the day and night. I only hope it's worth his while.'

Lorena couldn't help the mischief in her voice as she retorted, 'You love his records, so don't deny it!'

'Well, yes, I do, which is funny because they're not my type of music at all. Too modern, but he's got something worth listening to.'

'It will be funny to listen to the one he's working on now and think that some of the songs were composed here.' Lorena held tomatoes under the tap before wiping them dry. 'Do you think we'll be able to recognise them?'

Peggy shrugged. 'Who knows? How long does it take to get a record on the market?'

'Goodness, I don't know. Six months, perhaps?

I mean, they have to record things and that takes a while, doesn't it? and then get the record printed and distributed. It must be quite a long process.'

'Ah well, we'll know when his next one comes out. Lorena, will you take this lot down? Sel is deep in the entrails of the pump.'

'O.K.'

It was very important not to let Peggy see just how she was affected by Bourne Kerwood, so she took the basket with an air of affected coolness which would probably not fool that altogether astute lady one tiny bit!

The sun beat down through the trees, marking the ground with coins of hot gold. One pohutukawa had burst into flower and the bees were busy among its flowers. Soon others would join it and the headlands and bays would be marked by great splashes of primitive, glistening colour.

Lorena's heart did an odd flip when Bourne Kerwood emerged from the shade, his expression alert and interested, as though he had waited for her to approach.

'What have you got there?'

She smiled, meeting the open pleasure of his appraisal with as much frankness as she could summon.

'Peggy thinks you're in imminent danger of starving.'

'So she's despatched her handmaiden with provisions. Here, give it to me, and tell me about this fantastic tree.'

'The pohutukawa?'

'Yeah, the pohutukawa.' He stumbled with the pronunciation, then grinned. '*How* do you say it?'

'Po-hu-tu-ka-wa,' she enunciated clearly. 'Maori

is quite easy if you remember that the vowels are pronounced just as they are in Italian, that the consonants are exactly the same as for English except for wh, which is half-way between that and f, and the ng sound. "Sing *a*gain" gives you that.'

He hefted the basket. 'Thanks for the lesson, honey, but you don't pronounce the words exactly like that.'

Oh, but he was astute. Perhaps being a musician helped that acute ear for sound.

Rather foolishly Lorena returned, 'No, like most *pakeha* New Zealanders I'm inclined to be lazy. We're more conscious of the need to pronounce it carefully than we used to be, and I do try.'

'*Pakeha?*'

'A name given to New Zealanders of European descent. Nobody knows what it means, exactly, but it's used fairly widely.'

'Uh-huh. Where are you going?'

She blinked. 'Back to the house. I've delivered the basket and I do have work to do.'

'Don't snap at me,' he returned cheerfully. 'You're the most prickly girl I've ever come across, Lorena. Come down to the cabana and pick up the stuff from yesterday's basket, there's a good girl. And tell me about these trees.'

Not in the least averse to being with him for a little longer, Lorena walked beside him down the path. 'The pohutukawa grows in the north, as far south as Taranaki and Poverty Bay.'

A spurt of laughter escaped her when he turned a look of blankest incomprehension her way. 'Come again?'

'Half-way down the North Island,' she informed him.

'O.K., that I get. I've got a map. Why only there?'

'It doesn't like frosts when it's little, but it grows quite happily further south too—it just doesn't get there naturally. It will grow inland, but again, you've got to plant it. It's a sea-lover, and the only place it grows naturally is on the coast.'

'It's incredible. When I went over to that other island—Bounderman's, I think Sel called it—I saw one halfway down a cliff. I climbed down, and you'd never believe it, but the roots were right up at the top of the cliff—they spilled down the face of it and the foliage must have been almost a hundred feet down.'

'They're pretty tough. Mind you, they have to be. Living as they do is no picnic.'

He chuckled, then took a deep breath, as if savouring the lazy, salt-scented air. 'I like this place. When Aaron Read offered Waiwhetu to me I didn't believe a word of his description. He's a publicity man, so exaggeration is his business. But it's as beautiful as he said, and then some. I'm glad I came.'

'Which means, I suppose, that songs are coming freely,' Lorena observed, forgetting for a moment that she had decided to keep her defences raised and in good order.

A narrowed glance raked her profile, then he smiled. 'Yeah, pretty well. Tell me, Miss Prim and Proper, have you a boy-friend?'

Suspiciously Lorena wondered just what had brought this. But her fears seemed churlish, not to say foolish, so without giving herself time to think she answered, 'No, not at the moment.'

'I find that hard to believe,' he drawled, a disturbing note of intimacy colouring his deep tones. 'Are New Zealanders blind?'

'No.' She decided to make things clear; so clear that he could not possibly misunderstand her. 'I'm not ready for anything permanent, but unfortunately any boy-friends I've had have been keen on settling down. So—no go. I want to live a little before I get married.'

'I see.' He strode on for a few steps before asking, 'And what does living entail?'

'I've a degree to get. After that I want to use it to do research. And then I'm going to travel.'

With an odd inflection in his voice he said, 'You sound as though you have it all worked out. What if something interferes with your plans?'

'Such as?'

'Well, you could meet someone you fall for in a big way. What comes first then? Career—or love?'

She smiled a trifle smugly. 'I couldn't fall in love with anyone who wasn't sympathetic to my ambitions, so there would be no problems.'

'Oh boy!' His chuckle was soft, almost a taunt. 'Honey, you don't only look fifteen, you haven't grown up much beyond that. I wish I had that arrogant certainty you possess, but I'm afraid I lost it ten years ago.'

Her suspicions leapt into her eyes, darkening the glance she darted at him. Like everyone else she hated being laughed at, and there could be no doubt that he was enjoying some joke at her expense.

'Why?' she asked bluntly, thankful that they were almost at the beach house.

'Why? Because I realised that I couldn't have my cake and eat it too. I was eighteen when I had to come to terms with that.' He slanted a mocking glance down at her. 'A year younger than you. I wonder how old you'll be before you discover that you can't order the world to your disposal.'

Crossly she retorted, 'In your case it was different.'

He didn't pretend to misunderstand her. 'Only to a degree, certainly not in kind. I hope that your wonderful confidence in your own ability to control your destiny remains with you for the rest of your life, Lorena, but I doubt if it will. Maturity is the ability to pick the best options open to you.'

'You sound as if you think we're—well, playthings of fate,' she accused him.

Cynically, he returned, 'Honey, that's exactly what I do think. We don't have much choice, but what options we do have should be taken intelligently.'

Inside the beach house it was cool and dim, for the sun had not yet reached the wide-open sliding glass doors.

Without answering him Lorena went straight to the small kitchen and bar area, conscious of the fact that he was following close behind. As she unpacked the basket and put into it the dishes which he had emptied—and washed—she felt exasperation mixed with a rising tide of excitement, for he stood and watched her, and around the strong lines of his mouth there was a smile which mocked her attempts to put a barrier between them with her quick deft movements and air of efficiency.

At last, when her hands were stilled, she said uncertainly, 'Is that all?'

'Yes.'

'Then I'll go. Thank you for carrying the basket for me.'

At that he laughed, and took her hand and bent and kissed her, quite firmly but almost impersonally.

'Lorena, that air of quaint formality intrigues me. And you frighten the life out of me with your cast-iron armour and determination to do what you want. If I were your father I'd be worrying myself sick over you right now.'

The wild colour flooded her cheeks, but his last sentence startled her so that she lifted her downcast face, asking impulsively, 'Why on earth——?'

This time the kiss was every bit as firm but not in the least impersonal. For a moment Lorena felt a tide of panic which made her struggle convulsively, but his arms across her back were like steel bands, and after a moment the sheer expertise of the kiss got through to her and she found herself responding to his lips with a passion which sent every nerve in her body into singing life.

When he released her she moved away, her expression troubled, the shadowy green-gold of her eyes hidden by her lashes. One glance had told her that whatever had happened to her had not happened to him, for he looked frighteningly calm and that smile which was a taunt was back on the lips which had crushed hers into submission.

'That's why,' he said lazily. 'A girl like you is a challenge, Lorena.'

Defiance flamed into life. 'Are you so chauvinistic that you can't bear a woman with some independence?' she asked seethingly. 'Do you have to prove your superiority, even if it's only in strength?'

His laughter brought her temper to the boil. Small fists clenched, she turned to face him, hating him for his mockery and his arrogance, hating him more because he had shown her how little her much vaunted independence mattered compared to the practised lovemaking of a man who knew just how to elicit a response. Always it had been she who was in control of a situation; now she realised that she and her body could have widely differing ideas of the proper thing to do! And the realisation left her with a horrid empty feeling, as though he had cut away at the foundations of her life, leaving her poised uncertainly above an abyss.

'Calm down,' he drawled, the American accent emphasising his self-confidence. 'You'll explode if you let your temper ride you like that. And no, I don't have to prove my superiority in any way. I kissed you because I've been wanting to for some days now, and for that you can blame the fact that you flinch every time you come near me. And'—with a subtle change of inflection—'and the fact that you're very pretty and I like you—in spite of your efforts to choke me off as if I had the plague. Now, why not stop acting so outraged? If I'd been anybody else you'd have expected me to make a pass at you, wouldn't you?'

'Of course I wouldn't,' Lorena retorted, enunciating each word with cold scorn. 'I don't know how you act in your group, but I don't move in circles where I get swooped on just because I happen to be available—which I'm *not*!' she finished furiously, aware that she had spoiled the whole effect of her dignified speech with the last three words.

One black brow lifted in complete disbelief, but he said merely, 'O.K., I'll believe you. If you're so offended by what I found to be a very enjoyable kiss I suppose I'll have to apologise and promise never to allow myself to be beguiled into repeating it. O.K.?'

'Very well,' she said stiffly, feeling that somehow she had had the ground completely cut from beneath her feet, for to refuse to accept his apology—if one could call it that—would be to give the incident far too much importance. After all, she had been kissed often enough before, and with more passion, even if it hadn't been so well directed, she thought waspishly. And knew that she was blaming him for the betrayal her senses had inflicted on her.

'Well, that's that.' He touched her chin with his finger, tipping it up so that he could survey the mutinous expression she could not banish swiftly enough to escape his scrutiny. His glance sharpened, fixed on to her mouth, then moved with stabbing precision to her eyes. Lorena held her breath, saw for the first time beneath the façade of good looks and was shocked into something like fear by the turbulence she glimpsed there.

Then, as swiftly as a shutter falling, it was gone, replaced by the mockery which, she was beginning to suspect, was as much a mask as the lazy good humour.

'You'd better go,' he said curtly, releasing her with insulting carelessness, 'before your dragon comes steaming down here to rescue you.'

Chilled, yet relieved by his abrupt withdrawal, she turned to pick up the basket, saying with an attempt at lightness, 'Dragons smoked, they didn't steam.'

'So they did.'

Which left her with nothing to do but move briskly across the room and out into the dazzling sunshine, feeling as though she had been slapped in the face.

As she made her way up the path towards the house, swinging the basket angrily, she cooled down sufficiently to admit that she had deserved the rebuff. After all, she had acted as though he had tried to seduce her, accepting his negligent apology with reluctance and a rudeness which obviously angered him.

A shiver brought gooseflesh to her arms. For a moment she remembered the dark intensity of that stare just before he had let her chin go, the turmoil which she had barely glimpsed before he had turned away, and she could not help wondering just what the real Bourne Kerwood was like behind the screen he erected around his innermost being. No doubt a star had to learn to hide his emotions, but at what a cost! Perhaps, she thought wryly, the constant exercise of self-discipline was the cause of those celebrated temperaments—when the lid came off things really blew! She was convinced that when Bourne blew people ducked for cover, and bit her lip as she realised just how much she had provoked him by her gauche behaviour.

Yet he had no right to make casual love to her because she happened to be around. She wasn't Mount Everest, to be conquered just because she was there!

She was almost at the house when it occurred to her that perhaps he was married, and just entertaining himself with her. For someone who had vowed complete detachment her reaction to this thought was startling. The blood fled from her cheeks, leaving her shaken, almost faint, so that she had to lean against the trunk of a tree to recover.

Horrified by the power he seemed to possess over her, she pressed her hand to her mouth, her eyes uneasily surveying the sunlit lawn and vivid garden borders. She could not have fallen in love with him! The idea was preposterous. Attraction—yes, she owned candidly that physically he was very attractive, imbued with a virile masculinity which elicited a response from all that was feminine within her. But that was purely physical, a kind of chemistry which was based on no emotion, not even liking, certainly not respect or affection.

So it was stupid to think that he had any other power over her than the sensual. Which made it strange that the thought of him being married made her feel sick in her stomach.

A bird whistled idly from the leafy canopy above her. As if on cue Peggy appeared at the back door, a hand shading her eyes.

'Are you all right?' she called.

'Yes.' Grateful for the need to pull herself together, Lorena straightened up and moved towards her. 'Just admiring the view. It's a real credit to Sel, isn't it.'

It was a poor excuse, but after that first sharp glance Peggy appeared to take no further notice.

'Yes, it does look good. I think early summer is the time when everything looks best. Oh, Gordon rang. He wants to know if you'd like to go diving for scallops this afternoon with him and his cousin.'

Lorena chuckled, her own woman once more. 'He knows jolly well I don't dive. What he wants is someone to mind the boat while he and Mark dive.'

'Well, you might as well go. I could do with some fresh scallops and you won't be away for too long.'

The boys arrived almost immediately after lunch, Gordon rather diffidently presenting his cousin who was tall, a little older than him, and well aware of his good looks.

He made Lorena feel about fifty, although she noticed the appreciation in his eyes when she appeared. Fortunately he took his cue from Gordon and did not attempt to flirt with her, so that they soon slipped into an easy comradeship.

'You won't need anything to drink,' Gordon told her. 'Mum's packed enough food and drink to feed an army.'

'An army, perhaps, but not teenagers,' Peggy retorted, handing him a heavy basket. 'Lorena, have you got suntan oil and your glasses? It gets hot out there and you're not all that tanned yet.'

'I'm all prepared,' Lorena told her, warmed as always by the older woman's maternal enquiry. It was only when Peggy behaved so that Lorena realised what she missed by having no mother.

'Well, come on, then,' Gordon ordered, bossily male.

As they walked off down the drive Sel emerged from the pumphouse to ask, 'What's the limit for scallops?'

'Twenty per person,' Gordon told him promptly.

Sel grinned and retired once more to the fastnesses of the little building.

'Testing us,' Gordon told Mark, his deep baritone, so oddly at variance with his youthful appearance, disgusted.

'Yeah, man!' This off his chest, Mark became as high-spirited as the glorious day. 'Lorena, what's university like? That's where I'm headed year after next.'

'Oh.' She had wondered why he was up here before the start of the school holidays and now knew why. He had been accredited his university entrance and released early from school. Next year he would do his seventh-form year and possibly sit scholarship and after that start at 'varsity.

Feeling once more very old, she gave him her impressions of the university. The subject lasted them the entire length of the long drive and the short walk down the dusty road to the Haworths' farm boundary. From there a farm track led down to the small cove where they kept their runabout moored. Above the cove was the farmhouse, an old white-painted weatherboard bungalow dreaming amidst Mrs Haworth's beautiful garden.

Thoroughly used to the beauty around them, Gordon and Mark ignored it, packed themselves and Lorena as well as the baskets into the dinghy, and after a good-humoured squabble over who was best able to row, got them out to the runabout.

Once there Lorena stowed the food beneath the canvas canopy, smothered herself in sun cream and watched amusedly as they made a great thing of starting the outboard engine. Knowing full well that Gordon was capable of doing it blindfolded, she found Mark's attempts to show him what to do irritating, until she realised that he was showing off a little.

Not so far from being a little boy, she thought, hiding her smile and applying more oil with sudden intense concentration.

When they were off and outside the cove she steered while the boys wrangled over the diving gear. In spite of their adolescent spirits they were very careful to check it thoroughly, she noticed, as she manoeuvred the boat to get the bearings she needed to put them over the scallop beds.

'That big pohutukawa over there in line with the bluff on the island,' Gordon shouted.

Nodding, with the breeze whipping her hair into chestnut tails against her face, she bellowed back,

'And Beetson's red roof directly below Conical Peak, right?'

'Right!'

'O.K.'

Two minutes later saw the engine cut, the anchor heaved over and tested, and the boys getting into their kit. After hauling up the diving flag Lorena watched as they spat into their masks, pulled flippers on and fell over the side, clutching bags in which to store their loot. Then, with a sigh at the sudden quietness and peace, she took off her shirt and shorts to reveal her bikini, applied another layer of sunblock to her nose and lips and fished her book out of her bag.

But it would have needed something vastly more interesting than the book she was currently ploughing through—it was very *'in'* but also very dull—to keep her attention held on a day like this.

Perhaps, she thought dreamily, dipping her toe into the water, perhaps the Bay was truly an enchanted place, where dreams came true if you wished hard enough. Certainly it was incredibly beautiful, the water clear and sparkling green-blue, the hills lush with their spring growth of grass and behind them the blue-green of the range of hills which ran out to Cape Brett and the lighthouse marking the southern head of the Bay. And the islands! From where she sat she could see plenty of them, Motukiekie, Moturua, Urupukapuka and Redcap, and across the Bay, if she had binoculars, she would be able to see the Black Rocks, that strange volcanic reef which rose up so swiftly from the bed of the sea that the tourist launches could nose up to within inches of it. To the north-east was Mount Pocock on the Purerua peninsula, every ridge and gully outlined by the sun, a bold sentinel overlooking the entire Bay.

It was a harsh land, Lorena mused, then thought of the fertile farmlands inland, the pine forests of Waitangi, the huge citrus and sub-tropical fruit growing area around Kerikeri, and for 'harsh' substituted 'diverse'.

After long moments spent in admiration, she picked up her book, determined not to allow herself to be seduced into leaving it. She had promised herself that she would read it during the holidays, but she had little joy of it so far, for she didn't get time during the day and at night she was too tired to concentrate.

It seemed that the will to concentrate was lacking again. After a few moments when the print danced mockingly in front of her eyes she set the book down with a sigh. Like an idiot she had allowed Bourne Kerwood's moody good looks to intrude, and once there in her mind his features would not go away. Nor would that horrible query as to whether or not he was married. Somehow, she thought drearily, what hurt—hurt? no, what *grated* was not so much the thought of him being married—after all, what did it matter to her whether or not he had a wife?—but the fact that if he was, he was no better than a common philanderer.

And how's that for a bit of muddled thinking? she demanded of herself, angry at her stupidity. Really he was getting to be far too much on her mind. She would *not* give in to the promptings of a desire which was rather degrading because it was based only on her body's response. Old-fashioned thinking, no doubt, but she had been imbued with old-fashioned values by her parents, and somehow their deaths had imposed a kind of covenant on her. Besides, she owned honestly, those of her friends who had affairs seemed no happier than those who abstained. In fact, free love, whether consummated in affairs or by living together, seemed to cause far more grief than joy. Of course, there were marriages which were unhappy, too, but Lorena felt that those who married made a commitment and had the greater hope of happiness for it.

Her thoughts were drawing her into an area she instinctively distrusted, so that it was with a feeling of relief that she saw the strings of bubbles which heralded the boys' reappearance.

They were jubilant, both bags full to the limit allowed.

'Mum has a good way of cooking them with white wine,' said Mark, as he stripped his wetsuit from his body. 'How does Aunty Dot do them, Gordon?'

'I like them best just fried, but sometimes she does fancy them up a bit. How about you, Lorena?'

'Any way is lovely. Ready to go now?'

'Let's have something to eat first.' Gordon, hauling out the hampers, set to with Mark to demolish the contents with a gusto which proved how arduous scallop-hunting was. Lorena sat on the stern, drinking lime juice, as she looked around her with eyes which were half-closed against the glare, soaking in the sun with sybaritic pleasure.

She took little notice of the runabout until the sound of its engine as it was throttled back caught her attention. It was a hundred or so yards away, the Waiwhetu craft, except that it was not Sel who was at the wheel.

'Who's that?' Gordon asked.

'Oh, our guest.' Stifling a feeling of excitement

which seemed to have its origin just below her ribs, she waved. Bourne waved back, then pointed to the diving flag which still flew.

'Oh—crikes!' Swiftly Gordon moved to haul it down while Mark and Lorena both made gestures signifying that its being there was an oversight.

'Who is he?' Gordon muttered.

'Bourne Kerwood, but he doesn't want it known around the Bay.' She felt oddly guilty about giving his name, but after the first incredulous moment both boys' innate practical good sense asserted itself.

'So it is,' Mark said in awestruck tones, then reached over the side, fending the Waiwhetu boat off.

'Use the proper fenders, clunk!' Gordon roared, making Mark flush as he jerked the plastic foam fenders over the side.

Bourne cut the engine and grinned, obviously thoroughly at peace with his world, his dark eyes challenging and devilishly assured as he slung the anchor out.

'Hi, Lorena,' he said blandly. 'Care to introduce me to your boy-friends?'

The introductions were brief, both boys hiding their avid interest behind a polite and noncommittal mask.

Bourne eyed the open hampers. 'Do you think there could be anything left for me in there?'

'Help yourself,' Lorena offered coolly, suspicious of his motives in searching them out.

'There's plenty there,' said Mark, recovering somewhat from actually being in the same cockpit as a super-star.

Far from allaying Lorena's suspicions, Bourne's

subsequent behaviour increased them, for he set out to charm the boys and succeeded so wildly well that within ten minutes they were all gnawing chicken legs while they argued the best waves to surf and the best shellfish to eat.

Teenage boys were not, as Lorena well knew, the easiest of human beings to get on with, especially someone as sophisticated and worldly as Bourne. But he appeared to have no difficulty at all, and what made it so unfair was the fact that he didn't even appear to use charm; he was genuinely interested in them and they responded to him with unselfconscious respect and an equal interest. It was unfair because if he had used that approach to her she would know where she was, she reflected sourly, picking up one of Mrs Haworth's tiny cherry tomatoes and popping it into her mouth. But no, with her he was a creature of lightning changes of mood which left her quite defenceless—and with no sense of direction.

'How about you, Lorena?' he asked now, including her for the first time in the conversation. 'Do you like surfing?'

Gordon guffawed. 'She's just able to stay upright,' he answered for her. 'An expert, she is not. But put her on water-skis, and you really see something.'

'Really?' The dark bold glance slid over her slender body. 'Do you snow-ski?'

'Yes, when I can.'

'You'd like the Rockies, then. Colorado has some good fields—so have the northern states. Where do you ski here?'

'Ruapehu.' His look of dismay forced a smile from her. 'One of the three volcanoes that make up the middle of the North Island, south of Lake Taupo. You'd better have another look at that map.'

'They say the best skiing is further south,' Mark observed somewhat wistfully. 'At Coronet Peak and some of the new fields in the Southern Alps like Mount Hutt. They have a longer season down there, of course. One of these days I'll get there.'

'In the meantime you have a lot to do here,' Bourne said. 'Diving, swimming, surfing—what else?'

'Tramping,' Mark told him. 'And Gordon is a bit of a yachtsman. And of course if you're a history addict you can do the local spots, Waitangi and all that. This is more or less the first place where Europeans came to in New Zealand, you know.'

'Sealers and whalers, then missionaries,' Lorena and Gordon chanted in unison.

'Take no notice of them,' Mark said kindly. 'That's how we were taught history in the primary school, and like all clichés it's perfectly true. The whalers and sealers were the first here, and between them they made the Bay of Islands a place called "the hellhole of the Pacific". Then the missionaries came and tried to clean it up. That was—oh, twenty years or so before the Treaty of Waitangi, which saw the place finally signed over to England's protection by the Maori chiefs,' he concluded triumphantly to catcalls from Gordon. 'And you shut up, Haworth. Just because you're as thick as two boards together it doesn't mean others have to be!'

A challenge like this couldn't be ignored, of course. Lorena ducked as Gordon, slightly heavier than his cousin, tried to heave him overboard, only to slip and go flying over himself. Mark yelled with sheer high spirits and followed him over; the wildly rocking boat steadied somewhat, leaving Bourne looking at her with an enigmatic smile.

'Do you know as much as Mark of the history of the place?' he queried.

'Everyone does. Our European history is pretty short, so we revere it.'

Dark eyes measured her face, then, as the boys broke the quietness with exultant whoops, he bent to pick up an early plum.

'Nice boys,' he said, nodding towards them. 'But all of that energy makes me feel old.'

CHAPTER FOUR

THE scallops were delicious served as an entrée with sherry sauce, although as Sel remarked, he didn't think they needed sauce to enhance them.

'I like trying things out,' Peggy answered mildly, 'Are you swimming tonight, Lorena?'

'Yes. Why?'

'I just wondered. I suppose it's safe enough for you to swim by yourself.'

Lorena stared. 'Of course it is. What put any other idea in your head? I've been swimming by myself every evening since I came up here.'

'Oh, something that Bourne said.'

'Indeed?' Lorena knew that her eyes were sparkling, but could not prevent them from revealing her anger. Hastily getting to her feet, she took her plate across to the counter.

After a few moments of silence she managed to say in a voice devoid of feeling, 'I'm not silly, and if I got cramp so badly that I couldn't swim I think I could yell loudly enough for someone to hear.'

Peaceable Sel stated, 'He's right, in a way. It isn't a good thing to swim alone, but I don't think we need worry. This is a pretty sheltered area, so it's not as though you're in any danger from rips, or waves. About the only thing you do have to worry about is cramp, and as you say, you could raise one of us quickly enough.'

'Yes, you're a strong swimmer,' Peggy decided, and there the matter rested.

But Lorena carried her anger at Bourne's unwarranted interference as she marched defiantly down the track to the beach. Not only had he deprived her of her favourite cove, but it was clear that he didn't want her swimming at Waiwhetu beach itself. Such nerve, when he had the pool to splash around in, so he didn't really need the beaches at all!

Grumpily she pulled off her towelling coat, slipped off her thongs and set them on a rock beneath one of the overhanging pohutukawas. It was still bright sunlight, but the temperature had dropped from the heat of midday and the light was golden rather than the fierce whiteness of the sun at its zenith. No breeze ruffled the smooth waters of the Bay or set whispering the leaves of the trees on the point.

Gradually the loveliness and peace of the evening calmed Lorena's turbulent emotions. After all, what did it really matter? Compared to last year's guests Bourne was almost ludicrously easy to look after! And the fact that he couldn't be ignored like last year's lot was surely her fault, not his. He impinged too strongly on her, but there was no sense in getting herself so worked up about him.

By this time next year, she decided, as she made her way into the cool silken water, I'll be laughing at myself for getting into such a tizz.

Never having suffered it before, it had taken her a long time to discover that infatuation could be something which just happened, but she was not such a fool as to think that it could not be curbed by the application of large doses of common sense. No doubt Bourne saw her as someone to while away a few pleasant hours with; he was spoilt and probably his masculine charisma had made his conquests too easy, so that her refusal to behave like other women intrigued him just a little.

Which didn't prevent him from behaving with a highhandedness which irked her so much that it was all that she could do to keep her temper.

'Drat the man!' she said aloud, expressing her disapproval of the fact that even now he was coming between her and her pleasure with a defiant spurt down the length of the beach in her best crawl.

Half an hour later, when the air had become suddenly cooler and the sky was beginning to colour a soft tangerine in the west, she walked up on to the sand, pushing the strands of dark chestnut hair back from her face.

It was no shock to see him on the rock which held her clothes; some innate awareness had told her that he was watching her, but it did surprise her that he held out her wrap for her.

After one fleeting glance at the hard anger of his expression, she shrugged herself into the soft terry-towelling, carefully tying the belt with fingers which suddenly felt very stiff.

Still he said nothing, so that she slid her sandy feet into the thongs with a determination not to be the first to break the silence.

Like a couple of kids, she thought, half amused, determined not to lose face.

When he did speak his voice was flat as though he was subduing some strong emotion.

'Didn't Peggy tell you you shouldn't swim alone?'

'Yes.'

'But you took no notice of her.'

'Look,' she said as calmly as she could in the face

of the cold condemnation of his voice, 'I'm a big girl, Mr Kerwood.'

'You can't put me in my place by going all formal,' he returned coldly. 'Use my Christian name. And you know damned well that swimming by yourself is courting danger.'

Lorena gave the belt of her wrap a sudden tug, hauling it tight around her slender waist. 'Danger from what, for heaven's sake? We don't get sharks here, there are no currents or rips, and I don't get cramp.'

'Come here,' he ordered harshly.

When she made no movement to accompany him he took her by the shoulders and turned her, his controlled anger running through his fingertips to her shoulders. 'Head over there and tell me what you see.'

'Over there' was a patch of sand in a low reef of rock which ran from the cliff down to the sea. On the pale gold of the sand was a mound of lilac, a beautiful thing which looked exactly like the jellies Lorena's mother used to make for birthday parties when she was young.

'Jellyfish!' she exclaimed, moving over to get a closer look at the lovely, domed thing.

'Don't touch it!'

Shaken by the urgency of his command, she drew back quickly.

'Is it poisonous?' she asked carefully.

He shrugged, the anger apparently gone, and came across to stand beside her. 'I don't know, but there are jellyfish which can make you pretty sick. The sea out there is full of those things.'

Soberly she turned to look at the limpid waters of the bay. A shiver touched her skin at the thought of finding herself stung and in pain, possibly unable to make it back to land.

'I've never heard of anyone being stung by a jellyfish,' she said uncertainly, eyeing it with wary interest.

'I have,' he told her grimly. 'What would you do if you got one of those wrapped around that slim neck?'

'Have hysterics.'

'Hardly a sensible way of coping with the situation,' he said on a dry note, 'but at least you'd probably be heard. Now do I have your promise not to swim alone?'

'Oh!' She cast him a look of goaded fury, then hesitated. 'Oh, I suppose so, but I honestly don't know why you bother! It simply means that I can't swim!'

'I don't see why not. Why not use the pool?'

She shrugged. 'That's not for the hired staff.'

He laughed at that, and turned her around towards the track up to the house. 'If you keep hauling on that belt you're going to break yourself in half. I hereby give you permission to use the pool any time you like. But if it grieves you to give up the sea, why not ask Peggy or Sel to come with you?'

'They don't *swim*!' she explained, trying to prevent the laughter which seemed to be bubbling to the surface from a source deep within. 'I don't know for sure, but I think that deep inside Peggy believes that if God had intended us to swim He would have given us scales. And I've never seen Sel set foot in the water.'

Again he laughed, warm and companionable beside her. 'In that case I'll swim with you myself.' Perhaps he felt her become stiff beside him, for he went on casually, 'Or it's no go, honey.'

'You're infuriating!'

He shrugged. 'Put it down to over-developed protective instincts—and some heavy doses of propaganda from the Water Safety Council. You're a pretty good swimmer. Where did you learn?'

'In the Tepid Baths in Auckland.'

Without trying she could remember those occasions so well, the big pool, the hearty young instructor no older than she was now, and encouraging her to his utmost, her father. Odd how a chance remark could recall such a vivid moment from the past.

With the memory came the poignancy of grief. Swiftly steadying her voice she continued, 'My father took me along before he died, and I used to practise at a little beach not far from home.'

'Only child?'

'Yes.'

'I have a sister and a brother,' Bourne remarked companionably as though some of her grief had been revealed to him and was understood. 'Liz is married to a teacher while John is a lawyer. They both live in Chicago.'

'Is that where you come from?'

'Fairly close.' He slanted a mocking sideways glance at her. 'And if you mention gangsters I'll forbid you to swim at all!'

Oddly breathless, she managed to retort airily, 'I had no such intention. Do your parents live there?'

'No, they're farm people from Michigan—dairy farmers. So New Zealand is a little like home, though we don't have the small deer-like cattle you have here.'

'Jerseys?'

'That's it. We have Holsteins.'

'I think we call them Friesians here. They're used a lot for town supply.'

He grinned. 'You sound startled. Does the idea of me milking cows surprise you?'

'Not really.' And indeed, he looked competent enough to do anything he turned his hand to. Frighteningly competent, in fact. Lorena had always thought that musicians were somewhat vague people with brains full of harmony and not much else. Bourne had been a bit of a surprise. Apart from revealing an incisive keen mind, he handled the runabout as well as Sel, and she had heard him discuss the disadvantages of gardening by the sea with all the confidence of a man who knows what he is talking about. Understandable if he had grown up on a farm.

Now he said reflectively, 'Those cows were my first audience. My father swore that they gave more milk when I sang to them, so I sang as I helped him—how I sang! Every song I could think of, and when I ran out I made up my own.'

'What happened when you left?'

He laughed. 'Pop got a radio and they milked just as well to that. Taught me that no one was indispensable.'

This was a new Bourne, one that she had not known existed beneath the sophisticate, the superstar who wore his success like an armour against the world. Rather wistfully Lorena thought that she and this new Bourne Kerwood could have had a lot in common if things had been different.

Aloud she said, 'Well, that's a lesson all the better learnt for being learnt early, as my mother used to say.'

'You sound as if you still miss her.'

'I suppose I do,' she returned, shrugging, uneasy at the knowledge that he had found out about her history. 'She hasn't been dead that long.'

'It was a tough start for a kid.'

It was a statement of fact, not an expression of sympathy, and she was grateful for the understanding which kept his voice almost impersonal.

Without expression she said quietly, 'I had them at the time I needed them most, so it wasn't too bad. And people are marvellous.'

'I can imagine.'

The dry tone combined with the meaningful glance he directed towards her made her flush and lift her chin, glad that they were almost at the house.

'You're a cynic,' she accused.

'Only partly. And you must be immensely naïve if you don't realise the effect you have on the male portion of your acquaintance. Are you?'

Cornered, she hesitated, then retorted angrily, 'I'm not naïve! I just happen to feel that personality is more important than looks—at least it is here, whatever it may be like in Hollywood,' she finished with nasty emphasis.

He laughed softly. 'Then what are we arguing about?'

'Oh!' With the tables turned most effectively she could only stammer, angry at the ease with which he had made her look silly.

Wickedly he touched her hot cheek with one slow, trespassing finger. 'Not that I'm at all immune to your more physical attributes,' he murmured, daring her to turn and run away from him. 'You're far too lovely to be overlooked, but I think I like making your eyes sparkle like yellow sapphires as much as I like this. . . .'

His mouth was soft, almost tentative, against her eyelids, sealing them closed. Lorena felt her heart swell within her breast, threatening to block her throat with its beating, but although she thought, 'This is madness,' she made no attempt to pull away, caught in the dark spell that he seemed to be able to weave about her whenever he willed it.

His hands on her shoulders were gentle but firm, pulling her close against him as if he thought that she might try to escape. Every nerve sang, every sense became heightened, so that she could hear as well as feel the sound of his heartbeat against her, smell the faint trace of aftershave imposed on the clean male scent, feel the slight roughness of his cheek and chin.

'You look frightened,' he whispered, his mouth at the corner of hers.

'I am.'

'Why?'

'Because this is just asking for trouble.'

A thread of amusement touched the deep tones. 'And you try to avoid it?'

'Yes.'

'It's too late. Lorena——'

She opened her eyes, saw his as dark pools of laughter and desire and felt panic, then a delirious onrush of emotion which drowned all else as his mouth closed on hers.

Lorena had felt the impetuous rush of passion before, but the response that he kindled from her body left her gasping and breathless with its mindless urgency, so that she was caught like a toy in a whirlpool of emotion which left her almost completely defenceless.

He did not even try to disguise the satisfaction in his eyes when at last he lifted his head, but shamed at the open display of ardour which had encouraged her to press herself against him as if she never wanted them to be parted, Lorena pulled away while sudden tears enhanced the golden turbulence of her glance.

'You *are* naïve,' he mocked gently, pulling her back to rest against him. 'Or perhaps inexperienced is a better word. Why be ashamed of a perfectly natural reaction, honey? Haven't you ever heard of the chemistry that constitutes attraction?'

'Of course I have,' she said, furious with him for the effect he had on her, but more angry with the weakness which meant that she threw away every principle and scruple and hard-headed piece of advice she gave herself whenever he wished to amuse himself by making mild love to her.

'So why act as though I've forced you into bed with me?'

A flood of colour chased the pallor from her skin.

'I'm not!' she snapped.

He grinned mockingly, one finger tilting her chin so that she had to droop her lashes to prevent his too-penetrating scrutiny from seeing more than she wished.

'You puzzle me,' he mused. 'I think you're afraid of losing control, which is why you've done your best to give me the cold shoulder ever since you came.'

'And that irritates you?' Sudden scorn deepened her voice, gave light to the clear amber of her eyes. 'Perhaps I don't like you enough to wish for intimacies.'

He laughed at that, flinging his head back without releasing her so that she felt his amusement with every fibre of her being and wondered dazedly how laughter and passion could become mixed together into a response which frightened her by its urgency.

'Liar! We took one good look at each other and knew that this was inevitable.'

Resentment at the arrogance of the statement made her stiffen in his embrace. 'That, I suppose,' she retorted frostily, 'was why you were so nasty to me when we first met?'

'Did that rankle?' He sounded amused, completely confident, adding to the torch of her anger. 'Actually, yes. I wanted no diversions.'

'What changed your mind?' she asked sweetly, conscious of a cold chill somewhere around the region of her heart.

He bent, dropped a teasing kiss on the tip of her nose and set the seal on her misery by returning with a slow smile, 'Fishing for compliments? You did, honey. You've got something that sticks in my mind.'

It was all that Lorena could do not to bring up her knee and hurt him—severely—just as her father had taught her many years ago. But dismally conscious that her own ardour and the ease with which she had fallen into his arms probably had a lot to do with his calm assumption that she was ripe for a pleasant interlude, she held back.

For a moment head warred with heart. Would it be so terrible to fall in with his wishes, have a holiday affair and then end it, no bones broken? It was the sophisticated way to behave. Almost she relaxed in his arms, lulled by the desires of her body into acquiescence, when her guardian angel impelled her eyes upwards to meet his.

And she remembered what had been so obvious right from the start! Bourne Kerwood was a dangerous man, far too worldly for someone like Lorena Tanner. He was already anticipating her surrender, for his glance was lazily confident, as though he was quite happy to spend some time in pleasant dalliance until the need he knew how to arouse impelled her willy-nilly into his arms and his bed.

A horrible word she had seen used often in connection with pop stars imprinted itself on her brain.

Girls who pursued their idols, offering them their bodies, were known as groupies, an ugly expression, but one which suddenly seemed applicable to her. Was that how he thought of her, one more on the list? Deep within his eyes she could see a shimmering flicker of fire, the lust which only needed her acquiescence to fan into a blaze which would lead to nothing more than a pleasant interlude for him—but for her, the kind of degradation she had never thought to face.

Stiffly, like someone sleepwalking, she pulled herself away. Caution warned her that to fly at him would be stupid, to tell him her reasons for refusing to fall in with his wishes would only lead to the redoubling of his efforts. Adulation had spoiled him, and there was enough of the hunter for him to enjoy the chase, perhaps even enjoy making her fall in love with him against her will. Better to keep him at arm's length, make sure that there were no more opportunities for him to kiss her.

'What's the matter?' he asked quietly, that dark gaze never leaving her face.

Forcing her voice into lightness, she said, 'Sel and Peggy will be sending out a search party if I don't get back soon.'

'No doubt,' was all that he said, but she recognised the thread of amusement in his voice and felt her anger rush in, sweeping away the desolate feeling which had threatened her heart.

It would, she vowed silently as she walked across the smoothness of the lawn beside him, do him the world of good to find that someone in this world had no intention of giving in to him. He was too arrogant and conceited for his own good, and the sooner someone took him down a peg or two the better it would be for his character.

So sure was she of the desirability of this course of action that it never occurred to her to wonder why she felt so strongly about him—or what that odd ache of something perilously close to sadness meant.

That night was perfect for star-gazing, for the moon was past the full, at exactly the right stage for an intensive examination.

Lorena rang Gordon, arranged for him to come with Mark to pick up the telescope and the tripod and help her take them to the hill at the back of the Haworths' homestead.

Unspoken, barely acknowledged at the back of her mind was the thought that the boys' undemanding company would help her forget Bourne's provocative presence. And there was nothing like star-gazing for soothing the nerves and bringing home a realisation of one's insignificance in the scheme of things.

Peggy presented them with a basket, asked, 'Have you got a lantern? Not that one of yours, Lorena, with the red cellophane over it, I mean one that you can see with.'

'Yes, I've got a big one.' Mark flourished it before handing it to Lorena. 'Here, you take it and I'll get the tripod. Boy, it's a weight!'

'It had to be,' Gordon told him loftily. 'Otherwise it's no good. Ready, Lorena? Put the gear into the 'rover.'

Aware of the weight and bulk of the tripod and to a lesser degree the telescope itself in its case, Mr Haworth had lent Gordon the somewhat battered Landrover which was used for farm work. It smelt of sheep, dogs and various indescribable scents. Mark braced himself in the back with the wicker basket which contained the food and the tripod. Lorena cuddled the telescope case to her as Gordon gingerly eased into gear.

It was temperamental, but faithful. After a few jerks it took them smoothly down the drive and across the rattly cattle stop, then down the winding road, along the mangrove beach and up the other side into Haworths' drive. Halfway to the homestead, Gordon turned into a gateway. Accustomed to the country way of doing things, Lorena climbed down, opening the gate and closed it after the 'rover had gone through.

'I could have done that,' Mark remonstrated when she climbed back in.

'You'd have had to disentangle yourself from the tripod.'

Gordon laughed. 'Passenger always deals with the gates, Mark. You know that.'

'As a general thing, yes.'

'Applies to women just as much as men.'

Gordon made his way across the paddock, taking things a little more cautiously.

At the foot of the hill he stopped the 'rover, switched off the lights and said cheerfully, 'From here in it's climbing. You take the 'scope, Lorena, and I'll bring the basket and your paraphernalia.'

In the days when the Bay of Islands was a great centre of Maori population the hill had been a fighting *pa*, a fortified eminence with great stockades of logs backed by deep pits in tiers up its side. Now the stockades had gone, the pits were almost filled in and the descendants of those barbaric, heroic people lived much as everyone else except for the Polynesian joy of life which marked their outlook, tribal warfare lessened to mild rivalry in dance and song competitions.

It was a quiet place, the only sound the shriek of a pukeko down in the swamp. Lorena grinned as Mark demanded to know what that was, then refused to believe it when Gordon told him.

'Those lovely blue-purple birds, a bit like a bittern with red beaks and a habit of flicking a tuft of white feathers on its tail at you? Come off it!'

'Well, that's the noise they make,' said Gordon.

'Crikes, it sounds like a soul in torment. It's a super night, isn't it? Are we here?'

'Yep, we're here.'

'Good. I'm hot, lugging that great thing up a precipice. Why does the base have to be so heavy?'

'Think,' Gordon advised him with kindly condescension as he went to work in the light of the lantern to set the tripod up.

'So it doesn't wobble,' his cousin retorted, grinning. 'Can you manage the telescope, Lorena?'

'Yes.'

Always she enjoyed setting it up, adjusting the tube with its smaller starfinder telescope beside it, checking that the lens was in. From behind Mark asked questions, which Gordon answered as best he could, occasionally referring to her when he was stuck.

'It's only a baby,' she said in answer to one question. 'A sixty-mm refractor, to be exact. There, now take a look at that!'

There was a moment of silence as Mark, his eye to the lens, muttered, 'I can't see anything,' and then, 'Oh—yes! What is it?'

'The Great Nebula in Andromeda. They see it a lot better in the Northern Hemisphere. It's the most distant object you can see with your unaided eye.'

'Wow! How many light-years away is it?'

Lorena chuckled. 'Haven't the faintest, but Andromeda is one of our companion galaxies.' She turned and pointed low to the south. 'See those blurry things over there? Those are the Magellanic clouds, other companion galaxies. Later on we'll get a better view of them. But I'll find you a globular cluster. They're in our galaxy, but a long way from the centre of it. They're huge clusters of stars.'

The evening passed pleasantly. Mark was fascinated by the skies and spent much of his time peering at the book Lorena used as a reference, using the lantern with its layer of red cellophane to prevent night blindness.

Gordon was more of a dilettante in his approach, intrigued by the telescope rather than by what he saw through it, but between the two of them they kept Lorena busy answering questions. At last, when the little native owls were calling, 'More-pork, morepork,' from all around, and the food had been demolished, they decided to pack up, leaving the magnificent procession of the heavens to solitude.

They were almost at the house again when Gordon exclaimed sharply, 'What's that?'

'What?'

'Look—over to the north-east. Hell, that's a parachute flare! Someone's in trouble out beyond the bay.'

He jammed on the brakes, and both boys leapt from the 'rover as soon as it was still. They crashed through the trees to a clearing while Lorena ran down the drive, forgetting the telescope, forgetting everything but the fact that out to sea there were people in danger.

She flew into the darkness of the house like a bee heading for its hive, hammered on the door of Sel's bedroom and ran swiftly through the house to where Mr Read—bless him—had a pair of huge binoculars set up in a small summerhouse with a clear view of the sea.

With a swiftness surprising in one of his bulk Sel was beside her, pulling a shirt on over his bare shoulders.

Lorena stepped aside. Another flare shot high into the air to hang suspended, glowing crimson as a dying sun.

'Out beyond the Pin,' Sel muttered, his eyes to the binoculars. 'Can't see a bloody thing. What on earth could they be up to? There's no wind, no sea to speak of——'

'Trouble?'

That was Bourne, all the laziness gone from his voice. Lorena moved aside, absurdly aware of him in the scented dimness of the little building.

'Looks like it.' Sel straightened. 'It's not fire, as far as I can see. We'd better get out there—I'll take the launch. Lorena, ring the police in Russell and tell them what we've seen. I'll get Peg to put up clothes and food.'

'I'll come with you.'

Sel didn't argue, possibly aware that the grim note in Bourne's voice meant that no refusal would be accepted.

'O.K., Lorena, you'd better come too. You've got a St. John's certificate, haven't you?'

'Yes.'

'Right. Go and help Peg, then bring the stuff down to the wharf. Make sure you've got something warm to wear.'

The police at Russell had already heard of the flares. 'Yes; tell Sel we'd be grateful if he'd go—he'll have a start on us which may make the difference. The Haworths are taking their launch out too. You've no idea what it is?'

'No, except that we can't see fire.'

The constable's voice expressed frustration and concern.

'They've sent no distress signals. O.K., and thank you.'

CHAPTER FIVE

INCREDIBLE that such a beautiful night should hold drama and danger at its centre. As she stared at the whiteness where the water foamed away from the bows of the big launch, Lorena shivered, wondering what lay ahead.

Not too far away the Haworths' *Moana* sped on a parallel course. Occasionally Sel spoke into the radio keeping contact with them. It was Gordon who was manning their end, his voice excited yet oddly mature.

'Tell Lorena her 'scope's O.K.,' he said, and Sel passed the message on.

'Is that what you were doing?'

Lorena looked up at the dark shadow which was Bourne, tough and competent in a dark skivvy and a pair of jeans.

'Yes. We were just about home when we saw the flare.'

He smiled. 'I'd have thought they were a bit young for you.'

'Oh, don't be silly!'

His chuckle seemed to hang in the air as he moved back to stand beside Sel. Lorena looked again in the first aid box, checking carefully once more to see that there was enough stuff to cope with burns. She knew, as well as Sel did, that almost the only thing which could bring a craft to grief on a night as still and calm as this was fire. And although she had taken a St John Ambulance course, she could not help feeling fear at the thought of what might be facing them out there. Bad burns were so horrifying to cope with. Holding her fingers crossed, she checked once more, aware that if anyone was severely burned there was almost nothing that could help except the full resources of a hospital.

'The doctor is on the police launch,' said Bourne.

'I'm glad.' Decisively she snapped the first aid box closed, standing up so that she was on equal terms with him.

Or as equal as terms could be when he was six inches taller than her!

'Worried?'

'Yes. It must be fire.'

'Not necessarily. They could have hit a log, run aground on a rock, had a stay snap and be suffering from a broken limb, met the Flying Dutchman and be scared out of their wits——'

She laughed, as he meant her to, and felt gratitude for his understanding of her emotions.

'Hardly the Flying Dutchman—he doesn't operate in these waters. No, if they met anything it would be a *taniwha*.'

'Tell me,' he invited.

She whiled away the time by telling him about the *taniwha*, those creatures of water, usually villainous and man-eating but occasionally friendly, who held an important part in Maori legend and folklore.

'You have a talent for story-telling,' he said when she had finished. 'Do you write?'

She chuckled. 'Adolescent poetry. And children's books, which I never finish. I just play with it.'

'Given time, and the inclination, I'd say you'd do

it pretty well.' He spoke disinterestedly as though he had been asked his opinion and was giving it free from bias. Then the tone of his voice changed as the deep throbbing of the engines altered. 'Hullo, we must be almost there.'

They moved up to the wheel where Sel spoke to Mr Haworth this time. 'O.K.,' he said into the set, 'We'll cut engines and see if we can hear something. They should be around here—hey, Ted, can you see riding lights on the port bow?'

The radio crackled. 'Yes, I can. About half a mile—that's her!'

Another flare hissed up into the air, exploded and hung there, sending its lurid crimson glow beneath it to illuminate a yacht forging towards Russell.

'At least it's not fire,' Lorena breathed thankfully as Sel spun the wheel over.

'What the hell *is* the trouble?' she heard Bourne mutter and knew that he, too, was worried at what they would find there.

It was bad enough, in all conscience. Only one man was conscious, the owner of the yacht, and he was almost at the end of his tether.

As she sprang on to the deck, medical kit in her hand, Lorena heard him, half sobbing, say something about carbon monoxide, and felt her hands go cold with fear. What on earth could they do? Oxygen would be needed.

Fearfully she knelt and felt for the pulses of the three recumbent bodies in the cockpit. Two, a woman and a man, were beating slowly but regularly, but the other woman's was barely there, a faint fluttering beneath her fingers, and there was no movement in her chest.

Without thought Lorena called on the training she had received and began rescue breathing, covering the woman's mouth with her own, breathing life-giving oxygen into the flaccid lungs.

Dimly she heard Sel speaking on the radio, his short, clipped sentences betraying his anxiety. The two boys, their youthful voices awed by near-tragedy into hushed tones, stood awkwardly beside the yachtsman who watched Lorena with a still intensity which told her that the woman she worked on was his wife.

After a few moments there was a stir of movement as they transferred the other two on to the Waiwhetu launch. When Bourne and the yachtsman came back for her patient Lorena stood, swaying. Perhaps she had some carbon monoxide from the sick woman's lungs, perhaps she was merely overwrought, but she staggered, her head suddenly light.

'You—Gordon—take my place!' It was strange to hear Bourne's voice crack like a whip, but his arm around her was secure and firm. 'O.K.?' he asked, after a moment.

'Yes, I'll be fine.' She was helped carefully into the launch and went at once to the woman she had worked on. The pulse was a little stronger, but there was still only a very slight movement of the lungs, and with dread, Lorena realised that for this one help might come too late. Once more she bent to breathe air into those poisoned lungs, but Bourne said crisply, 'I'll do it. You get up into the fresh air.'

Leaving the yachtsman seated by his wife, holding her hands as though willing her to come back from that no-man's-land she inhabited now, Lorena moved up the companionway into the wide cockpit where the two others were lying as if asleep.

'Will they be all right?' she asked Sel.

'I think so. I don't know much about carbon monoxide, but I'd say they were got out in time. It's the lass below we're worried about.'

'What's happening now?'

'Ted Haworth is going to take the yacht in tow to Russell. We're faster, so we'll get these there, meeting the doctor on the police launch half way. I've radioed to tell him what's happened, and he's already radioed for oxygen. We'll be met by a couple of ambulances at Paihia.' He lifted his hand to the Haworths and spun the wheel.

Like a great beast the launch lifted in the water, the deep roar of the diesel engines reverberating through the boat. Lorena drew in deep breaths of the fresh salt air, then turned and went below.

The yachtsman was talking, muttering to Bourne as he breathed life into the woman.

'It must have been the manifold,' he said now, hopelessly. 'But I had the whole thing checked over at the end of winter. God knows how it happened. I put the engine on when I saw there wasn't enough wind to get us in. They were tired, so they'd gone below quite early. God, if I hadn't gone down to make some coffee they'd have all died there. I'd have sailed into Russell on a death ship.'

'Then thank God that you did go below,' Lorena told him crisply, realising that she could not allow him to give way to his shock and anguish just yet. He would need all of his self-control. There was a note of hysteria in his voice which revealed how close he was to his limit. So she asked evenly, 'What's your name?'

'Name?' He stared, as though she was mad, then made a visible effort to pull himself together. 'Brian Miller, from Auckland. We—this is my wife Deirdre—we came up from Auckland with friends, Sally and Francis Webb.'

He was not very old, perhaps twenty-five or twenty-six; short and thickset with a day's growth of beard on a jaw which would normally be competent and somewhat jaunty. Now his eyes were red-rimmed, his mouth slack, and the skin which stretched tautly over his cheekbones seemed to have loosened, making him older and defeated.

Lorena felt sudden tears scald her eyes. His pain reached out to her, enmeshed her, so that she was swamped by his agony of fear and dread and bewilderment.

His wife looked barely older than Lorena, a plumpish little woman with fair hair and childish features made more so by the bright colouring of her skin, the dreaded cherry hue which was a signature of carbon monoxide poisoning.

Above her Bourne crouched, his dark head bent to hers in the monotonous rite of inhale, exhale, inhale, turn your head, exhale, and all the time watch for the reaction which would tell you that her lungs were working of themselves.

He looked more than competent, Lorena thought, her heart swelling with an absurd joy and gratitude. He looked demonic, as though he was determined that Deirdre Miller should not die. She had thought him hard and sophisticated; she was seeing another angle of him now, a Bourne who would not be defeated, who fought with uncompromising resolution an enemy he could not see.

'I'll take over now,' she said, after a few moments,

wondering why she should feel so happy in this atmosphere of tragedy.

'Check them upstairs.'

Meekly she did as she was told, discovered that the man was muttering beneath his breath but that his pulse was strong, almost normal, and his chest rose and fell regularly. His wife—Sally Webb—was not stirring yet, but her pulse and breathing were regular.

'Here's Summer with the doctor,' said Sel, breaking in on her thoughts. Sure enough, there was the police launch; in a few seconds it had drawn up beside them and Sel was talking to the big, burly constable while the doctor made a brisk inspection of his patients.

He seemed happy enough with the two Webbs, but his expression was grave when he came up from examining Deirdre Miller.

'We'll have to get her to oxygen as soon as possible,' he said. 'I suggest we leave them here, Sel, as you're just as fast as Summer. Head for Paihia.' He nodded to Lorena and disappeared backwards down the steps.

After a few moments Brian Miller came up, looked around hesitantly, then came across to where Lorena sat beside the two Webbs.

'The doctor and the other chap are working on her,' he told Lorena in a high, unnatural voice. 'I'm in the way. Oh—*God*! What'll I do?'

'You won't help her by giving way now,' Lorena returned unsympathetically. 'Look, we've rounded Tapeka Point. We'll be at Paihia soon, and the ambulances are waiting.

'I know.' He relapsed into a strained silence as the two big launches forged down the harbour to where the lights of Paihia gleamed along its three bays.

High on the hills the leading lights burned, showing the way into the little port of Opua; by turning her head slightly Lorena could see a few scattered lights from that upper end of the Bay, and over the water on its peninsula was Russell, asleep now beneath the vast, uncaring sky where Orion and the Cross turned slowly. The big hotel at Waitangi slept too beneath the historic patch of ground where Maori chiefs signed a covenant with Queen Victoria to bring them under her sovereignty. The Treaty of Waitangi. It had been breached often enough, but the spirit had been the basis for the excellent race relations which existed now.

Sally Webb stirred, her hand moving. Stooping, Lorena slipped cool fingers into her grasp, murmuring, 'It's all right now. You're all right. And so is Francis.'

'Frank. . . .' The word came soft as a dawn breeze.

'Frank is fine,' Lorena said loudly, then, 'Brian, you tell her.'

He came from the depths of his private hell to reassure the girl that her husband was alive and well. Perhaps the sound of his name called her husband back to consciousness, for he stirred and muttered again, his eyes half opening.

On an impulse Lorena put Sally Webb's hand into her husband's; it seemed to reassure both of them, for they relaxed and were still handfasted when the launches berthed at the wharf at Paihia and the ambulance men took over.

Lorena flattened herself out of the way, watching with compassionate eyes when Deirdre Miller was carried out on her stretcher, her pretty face covered by an oxygen mask. A strangled sound came from Brian Miller's throat; without a word he lunged away up the steps and into the ambulance.

'Do you think she'll make it?' It was a stupid question, but Lorena could not help asking it.

Dr Calder shrugged. 'Where there's life ...' he said. 'And she's hanging on. Thanks for your help, all of you. I think we can safely say that if you hadn't seen that flare and taken off so quickly she'd be in a lot worse way. I'll see you, Sel.'

'Do you want a lift back home?'

'No, Summer will give me one, thanks.'

'Cheerio. Bourne, will you let go for'ard? Go aft, Lorena.'

It was suddenly cold. Depression caused by tiredness swept over Lorena, making her shiver. Without exchanging a word with anyone she went below, pulled on a jersey and made coffee for them all, carrying up the mugs with infinite care. Brian Miller's anguished face kept presenting itself to her—so young, too young for tragedy. When Bourne asked her what she was thinking of, she told him, her tiredness robbing her of the defences she usually erected against his more probing questions.

'Nobody is too young for tragedy,' he retorted crisply. 'You should know that, Lorena.'

'I suppose so.' A yawn split her face. 'Excuse me,' she muttered, hiding her face in the coffee mug.

His chuckle was intimate. 'Such a meek answer must mean total exhaustion. Why don't you go and lie down?'

'We'll be home soon,' said Sel. 'Hardly worth your while, Lorena. You can sleep in tomorrow.'

Which was exactly what they all did, even Peggy who had waited up for them. The sun was high in the sky when Lorena woke to an insistent tapping at her window. Yawning, she climbed out of bed, pushed a hand through her hair and walked across to the screens, for she always slept with the window and sliding door wide open.

It wasn't Peggy who stood outside, but Bourne, clad in shorts and a thin cotton shirt, his narrowed eyes alight with laughter and mockery at the dismay in her expression.

'Wait——' Lorena stammered, disappeared back into the room. The nearest cover up for her flimsy nightgown was her beach coat; her dressing gown was far too transparent. As it was she felt that the towelling wrap revealed too much length of leg, but she didn't want to encourage his mockery by dressing.

'Hi,' he greeted her, his glance lingering on the tanned slimness of her legs, the vulnerable hollow at the base of her throat. 'You look a little like the morning after the night before.'

'I feel it.' A pulse flicked in her throat; he was too virile and masculine for her peace of mind and she did not like the bold appraisal in his eyes. 'Where do you get your energy from?'

'Like Churchill, I nap at odd times.' He laughed at her bewildered expression and held out his hand. 'Come on, come for a walk with me. It will give you an appetite for breakfast.'

Sternly repressing the bubble of excitement which threatened to overthrow the resolution she had made the day before—only yesterday, but it seemed so long ago!—she said, 'No, I can't.'

'Afraid?' he taunted, that knowing smile of derision curling his mouth.

'No,' she returned aloofly, perhaps with more curtness than was polite.

His features hardened into a mask of hauteur, then relaxed. 'So be it,' he said lightly, 'Behold me—bereft.'

She smiled. 'I don't believe that,' she told him drily as she turned to go back inside. A sudden thought struck her. Over her shoulder she asked, 'Have you had breakfast?'

'Solicitude? As it happens, no, but don't come over all little-womanish. I can manage for myself.'

There was no mistaking the cool note of disdain in those deep slow tones. Lorena bit her lip but managed to say calmly, 'Very well, then. If you do get hungry you know where the fridge is.'

'I do indeed,' he said softly, and turned and walked across the lawn, arrogant, uncaring, broad shoulders above narrow hips as he moved with the grace and lithe ease of an athlete.

Something peculiar happened to Lorena. She stood with one hand on the curtain, watching him as he walked away, drowned in a sensation of mingled sweetness and pain which could only be love. 'Dear God,' she whispered as her hands clenched the soft folds of the curtain. 'It can't be!'

But it was. Like a fool she had fallen in love with him, and for her there would be no escape from pain and disillusionment. For he saw her as nothing more than a mild holiday diversion while she knew that she would follow him barefoot across the world if he asked her.

Slowly, fearfully, she released the curtain and turned into the cool dimness of the room with movements which were mechanical, without their usual grace. And being Lorena, the first thing she did was scold herself for being so foolish as to lose her heart to someone who would treat it as a plaything. And just as typically, she felt gratitude that she loved, for even as she accepted the pain and heartache that would come of it she knew that in love there was fulfilment and enrichment which would help her become more of a woman, less a shallow girl.

As she showered and dressed she decided that Bourne must never know. With a wisdom which must have been a heritage from her female forebears, for it was certainly not based on experience, she knew that it would be the only way for her to emerge unscathed from this foolish love of hers. He wanted her; she knew that, just as he knew that she was acutely responsive to him. Doubtless he would think little of her scruples about an affair, and although she knew that he would not force her in any way, if once he realised that she loved him he would not take seriously her refusal to be beguiled by any flirtation.

With the rather shattering honesty that was one of her characteristics, Lorena owned to herself that her defences against his sensuality were pitiful and few; if he really desired her surrender was inevitable.

So it would be better for everyone, especially for her, if there was no possibility of surrender. Which reinforced her decision made fewer than twenty-four hours before not to allow any further intimacies.

Such independence should have made her feel strong and proud, but she was only conscious of a nagging ache deep within, which, she realised, she would simply have to get used to. If she gave in to her body's needs and desires the price she would pay in shame would be much higher than mere heartache.

As if her rejection of him had marked some point in their relationship she found that Bourne had changed in his attitude towards her. Gone was the half-teasing, half-derisive mockery that had so annoyed her. Instead he was aloof, the dark eyes hooded in enigmatic features. He looked, she thought with sudden perspicacity, rather like his record covers.

Just before lunch the Russell constable rang to tell Sel that Deirdre Miller was going to make it.

'Great news, Summer,' said Sel with evident satisfaction. 'How are the others? O.K.? Good. I'll tell Bourne and Lorena.' He listened for a few moments, a frown creasing his forehead, then said, 'No. He wants a holiday without publicity. You haven't—no, of course not. I'll ring the Haworths and make sure neither of those boys lets it out. Just check with the doctor, will you? I doubt if the name means anything to him, but you never know.'

This summary dismissal of Bourne's fame brought a twinkle of mischief to Lorena's amber eyes, already alight with delight at the news. Bourne, who had shared lunch with them, lost that look of faint hauteur for a moment in a grin which showed that he, too, appreciated Sel's unconscious put-down.

However, the amusement faded swiftly leaving him keen-eyed and alert, almost hard. 'Reporters?' he asked as Sel replaced the receiver.

'Yes. Summer hasn't told them who you are, of course, and he's going to make sure that the doctor doesn't mention your name. Lorena, hop across to the Haworths', will you, and put those boys on their honour not to talk to reporters.'

'I'll take you,' Bourne offered, rising swiftly. With a faint smile he went on, 'After all, it's my business.'

'The reporter from Russell will probably ring the Haworths to get their version of the incident,' Sel told him. 'But you never know. She may decide to come out and photograph things. And if the boys get talking to her—well, you are news.'

'I guess.' Bourne said noncommittally. 'Coming, Lorena?'

'Do you need me?' She met the cool scrutiny of his gaze and continued, less confidently, 'I mean—you can convince the boys without my help.'

Peggy got to her feet, putting bread and butter plates together with unnecessary and most unusual noise as Sel said, 'Go with him, Lorena. There's no need to keep regular hours today—we could all do with a rest.'

They took the runabout and went by sea. Bourne was very polite to Lorena, who was very polite back, uneasy because she did not understand him and was uncertain of how to react. At least, only partly. Her body reacted only too sensitively to his presence. She had not known before that desire could be a physical ache, a counterpoint to the ache in her heart, that the nearness of the man she loved caused a kind of delicious irritation to her nerves which made her restless.

'What's the matter?' he asked when they were halfway there, and she had moved from one side of the boat to the other. 'You're like a cat on hot bricks.'

'I don't know,' she lied, sitting down with the determination to remain there until they arrived at Haworths'. 'Tiredness making me jumpy, I suppose. I'm glad Deirdre Miller is going to recover.'

'Uh-huh. She's too young to die.'

'When I said that you bit my head off.'

He shrugged, slanting her a sardonic sideways glance. 'You said he was too young for tragedy. There's a difference. To die before you've experienced anything—that's the real tragedy.'

Lorena tried to be objective about things, but perhaps her own inner feelings showed in her comment. 'She's experienced love, surely that's something.'

'Love? I guess so. Love and sex—yes, she's had that. She's not had children, though; or lived long enough to gain wisdom.'

'Do you think wisdom comes with age?' Lorena couldn't prevent the note of scepticism in her voice. It seemed very odd that a man who owed his career to the adulation of the youth of the world should pay such respect to age.

'Surprise you? I'll qualify it, then. Some people are born wise, but most have to acquire what wisdom they do attain by painful experience, year after year of it. Even then, some die as foolish as they're born, but one of God's finest creations is an old person, a little cynical but tolerant and compassionate of others' foibles and weaknesses, because their experience has taught them that humanity, by and large, can always find excuses for their actions, whatever they are.'

'You're a cynic,' Lorena returned, shaken by the jaded note in his voice.

'I don't think I am—entirely.' He spoke slowly, to all intents and purposes concentrating on steering the runabout away from the coast. The sun struck sparks of blue from his dark hair, emphasised the hard strength of his features.

Lorena swallowed, looking away as he continued, 'But would it be such a surprising thing if I were? You can have no idea of what it's like to be an ordinary guy one minute, the ordinary son of ordinary parents, and then suddenly to be idolised, pandered to, sought after, as if you were the new Messiah. Believe me, honey, it's not good for the character.'

There was raw emotion colouring the deep slow tones, as if the real Bourne Kerwood was showing behind the mask he habitually wore.

Without stopping to think Lorena said, 'I can understand that. But you seem to have come through relatively unscathed.'

'Wishful thinking.' His smile was a travesty, a twisted, wry movement of his lips which expressed more than his words. 'Perhaps I was lucky. I had a good, solid childhood, full of all the old-fashioned basic values to back me up, but power makes you drunk. And an entertainer is more vulnerable than most to flattery and adulation, because that's what he wants—love and admiration and applause.'

'That doesn't sound like you at all,' Lorena said impulsively. 'You give the impression of being very self-sufficient.'

Shoulders lifted in a shrug which set at naught her words. 'Hard won, I promise you. Oh, it was delightful for a while—money to burn, the applause, the lights and the crowds screaming, the girls, all available and more than willing to please—and I took advantage of the whole lot. But deep down I didn't believe it would last, so I didn't lose myself entirely in the image. Even then, drunk with the excitement, I realised that the public is fickle, and if they turned against me the whole lot would collapse. And the first to go would be the girls, those lovely, loving girls. I saw other stars trying desperately to climb back to where I was—and I knew that that could happen to me too. So I remembered those roots of mine and made a deliberate decision that I would be true to them and use the opportunities I had for finding out what I really wanted to be.'

Lorena sat motionless, afraid to move in case he stopped talking, desperately clutching these moments of happiness to her. Other girls he might flirt with and make love to, but some instinct told her that it was very rarely that he spoke as openly as this of himself and his emotions.

But, as if wary of revealing any more of himself he said ironically, 'I seem to have caught the modern habit of self-analysis and baring one's soul to the nearest unfortunate recipient. You're a good listener, Lorena. I won't do it again.'

'I don't mind,' she muttered, turning her head away so that he couldn't see how shaken she was by the intimacy of the situation. Then, her voice changing, she cried, 'Look, Bourne, dolphins!'

They were beautiful, grey sleek smiling things. But they stayed only a few minutes before turning out towards the open sea, their humped backs breaking the water with barely a splash.

And then they were at the Haworths', and there was no further opportunity for any intimacy.

For the first time Lorena witnessed Bourne's effect on a member of the opposite sex other than Peggy. After five minutes she decided with some asperity that although his position as a star might have given him wealth and adulation it couldn't have added anything to his natural inbuilt expertise when it came to women.

Not that he set out to charm, or used any tricks, she had to own. He just had the knack of making any woman, even cheerful, practical Mrs Haworth, feel like a queen. Without antagonising any of the male Haworths, furthermore! The man had charisma, but it was firmly based on an inner strength and purpose which commanded respect—and would always do so, regardless of what happened to his career as a musician.

And she was quite prepared to bet that girls hadn't been any more willing and loving after his discovery as a star than they were before!

'You're very quiet, Lorena,' Mr Haworth remarked after his wife had poured them tea in the big, comfortable kitchen.

'She's tired,' said Bourne, adding with a spark of mockery, 'Late nights don't do her temper much good, either.'

'Snap at you, did she? She's got quite a temper when she's roused.' Gordon picked up a handful of yellow plums from the bowl in the centre of the table and set to polishing the bloom from them. 'Remember the time you threw the rock at me that first summer you came up, Lorena?'

'Horrid little beast that you were; yes, I remember.' Lorena pulled a face at him. 'I've often thought I should have thrown it to hit you.' She ignored his laughter, turning to say to Bourne and Mark, 'He was tormenting a crayfish on the beach, and wouldn't stop when I told him to.'

'I must have been a nasty little creep,' Gordon said reminiscently, demolishing the plums with effortless efficiency. 'Still, you made your point. That was two years ago, wasn't it? Will you be up here next year?'

Lorena shrugged, not willing to look that far ahead. 'Who knows?'

'I won't be.' Mark snatched a plum from Gordon as he announced, 'I'm going to be in Fiji this time next year. Mum and Dad are moving there in a few weeks' time, for Dad's promotion. I'll finish school here, then go across for a holiday. I don't suppose you'll be here either, Mr Kerwood.'

'It depends on a lot of things,' Bourne said blandly, 'but I wouldn't mind coming back. I don't need to tell you that the Bay is beautiful. I'd like to see something else of New Zealand. And would you like to call me Bourne? All this Mr Kerwood business puts me far too firmly into the next generation on.'

Gordon grinned somewhat bashfully, unconsciously giving away the fact that as far as he was concerned that was exactly where Bourne was situated!

Perhaps to cover up for her son's gaucherie Mrs Haworth said pleasantly, 'It's an unusual name, isn't it? Is it your real name or a professional one?'

'All my own,' he told her. 'Bourne is an old family name. My grandfather was Bourne Kerwood too. I've been told that Kerwood means something like "the dweller in the meadow by the wood", but I've never checked it out. Like you, we're of English stock. One of these days I'll find out where we came from.'

'How long have your family been in the States?' Mrs Haworth asked, her attention aroused by this reference to one of her interests, genealogy.

'Couple of hundred years, I'd say.'

She laughed. 'We tend to forget that America has been settled for so much longer than us. Here anybody who came out more than one hundred and fifty years ago was a very early settler.'

'Not counting Maoris,' said Gordon. 'Hey, Lorena, that 'varsity party is back at the *pa* up the coast. You know, at Rawle's Point. Want to sail up one day and take a look?'

'What *pa*?'

Lorena remembered that Bourne had been studying archaeology before fate snatched him into the limelight.

'It's a very old fishing *pa*,' she explained. 'The university digs up a little more each year. They think it's at least seven hundred years old, which makes it and the Mount Camel diggings at Houhora about the oldest sites in the north. It's fascinating.'

He nodded, but said nothing more about it. The conversation moved to last night's mercy dash, and Bourne explained his reasons for asking that his name be kept out of it. Both boys readily assented.

As Gordon put it, 'Really slack for you to have your footsteps dogged by screaming fans. Some girls would do anything for a sight of a real live star.'

Everyone laughed; after a few more minutes it was time to go.

If Lorena hoped for the same closeness on the way back she was disappointed.

'Nice people,' Bourne said casually, and that was about all that he said. The aloofness was back, and this time, it seemed, there would be no cracks in the barrier he erected between himself and the world.

CHAPTER SIX

THAT trip set the tone for the days that followed. Although he almost ceased to be a guest, eating most meals with them, Bourne treated Lorena with a remote courtesy which chilled and hurt her. And he spent much of his time in the beach house, working, no doubt, on his music.

Meanwhile Peggy and Lorena scoured the house from top to toe in preparation for Christmas, before embarking on an orgy of cooking.

'Mind you, it's silly the way we carry on,' Peggy commented one day as she and Lorena loaded a run of pies into the deep freeze. 'We exhaust ourselves before Christmas so that we won't have to work during the holiday, with the result that we don't enjoy it as much as we should do because we're too tired.'

'You wouldn't have it any other way,' Lorena teased, pushing a lock of chestnut hair back from her face as she handed the next plastic-wrapped offering.

'It's always been that way. I remember my own mother complaining of the work, but she hated it when we younger ones took over the cooking. She always made the pudding.'

'It seems silly to have a great heavy meal in the middle of summer. I'll bet a lot of stomach-aches can be blamed on tradition. I can understand our ancestors wanting to keep up the old ways—they were homesick. But you'd have thought that we'd have grown out of the habit.'

Peggy gave her a sharp but affectionate glance. 'Would it feel like Christmas to you without hot poultry and mince pies and plum pudding?'

Laughing, her expression alight with humour at being caught out, Lorena returned, 'No, of course it wouldn't. Don't worry, I love the whole thing!'

'What whole thing?'

Bourne's deep voice made both women start and turn to where he lounged in the doorway.

'What whole thing?' he repeated when nobody spoke, his dark gaze lingering on Lorena's flushed face.

'Christmas,' she said shortly, angry at the tumult his presence brought to the secret pathways of her being.

'Christmas?' He lifted his brows at her, openly mocking.

Perhaps Peggy felt the tension between them, for she said briskly, 'All of the work and fuss. Which reminds me, Bourne, Mrs Haworth rang. They're having a woolshed dance just before Christmas and she wondered if you'd like to go.'

Again that enigmatic glance swept Lorena's startled expression. She had accepted her invitation to the Haworths' pre-Christmas dance, a tradition in the district, but it hadn't occurred to her that they would ask Bourne too. And yet why not? The Haworths had accepted him at face value, and it would have been rude to leave him out. Now her heart beat double time at the thought of him going.

'They usually invite the people who stay on their beach, plus friends of Gordon's and their own—a lot of people all intent on having a good time,' Peggy told him, a little astringently. 'And the lights are somewhat subdued, so it's unlikely that you'll be recognised if you want to be incognito. It's strictly first names.'

He grinned at that, well aware that Peggy thought his desire for privacy slightly overdone. 'Are you going, Peg?'

'Yes, of course.'

Lorena laughed at this, casting a mischievous glance at the older woman. 'Peggy and Sel always give a demonstration of the Charleston, just to keep us younger ones in our place. They're fabulous!'

'Then I can't possibly refuse,' he said, smiling with lazy charm at Peggy, who thawed visibly. 'I'll go and let the Haworths know.'

But after a couple of minutes he was back, grinning. 'I cannot get this telephone system in my head,' he complained. 'A frosty-voiced female has just told me that Haworths are on my line. Would either of you like to translate?'

'You go, Lorena,' Peggy told her resignedly. So Lorena went, too conscious of the pain and rapture of her newly found love to be able to relax in his presence.

'It's quite easy,' she explained when they reached the nearest telephone. 'Haworths are on our party line and their number is "S" which is three short rings. You ask if anybody is working——'

'Just get them for me, there's a good girl,' he interrupted blandly, all warmth gone from his expression.

To her horror Lorena felt the threat of tears. He must not see how much he affected her! With a cheerful 'O.K.' which cost her more effort than a speech she lifted the handpiece, turning slightly so that he could not look directly into her face. A few surreptitious blinks disposed of any surplus moisture in her eyes, and when at last somebody answered on Haworths' end she said politely, 'Mr Kerwood would like to speak to you, Mrs Haworth,' and handed the receiver over with an air of cool efficiency.

It did not help to ease the hurt she felt when Bourne spoke to Gordon's mother with the same friendliness which he used towards Peggy and Sel. As she walked back towards the pantry where the deep freeze and the preserves were stored, she thought bitterly that Bourne Kerwood liked people to stay in the slots he assigned them to. As long as they did, he was pleasant to them. It was people like Lorena Tanner who refused to play the role given to her who saw the less amiable side of his character. For 'less amiable' read downright nasty, she thought, remembering the abrupt transition of mood she had witnessed.

He had wanted to put her in her place, and had succeeded with brutal swiftness. Like a fool she had thought that they could at least be friends, but it seemed as if he wanted nothing from her but the careless response of her body to his masculinity.

And that he was not going to get, she vowed fiercely, certain now that in spite of her weakness in falling in love with him she had had a very lucky escape. How easily she could have deluded herself into thinking that his pursuit of her must mean love of a sort; it would have been fatally easy to surrender to his experienced sensuality. Fatally easy—and she could have been left weeping when he went back to the States.

If anything had been needed to stiffen her resolve not to become his summer plaything, it was this incident when he revealed how very different was his outlook from hers. Love for him meant a game, a hunt which had for its satisfaction the assuaging of desire. Very sophisticated and modern, no doubt, but not for Lorena, who could think of nothing more shattering than a series of affairs leading to no more than the easing of a purely physical desire.

So she told herself that it was as well she had discovered how greatly their attitudes differed before she was badly hurt, ignoring the fact that her heart felt as though it was bleeding to death.

That evening, when he was safely at the cabana, she swam in the pool, then impelled by a mixture of emotions she could not disentangle, hunted through the record collection until she found Benjamin Britten's War Requiem and put it on the stereo player which the ever-thoughtful Mr Read had had installed in the garden room.

As she sat in her beach wrap listening to that splendid, poignant evocation of death, grief and sublime hope, the tears which had been denied during the afternoon came freely, washing away some of the humiliation and pain. While the tenor and baritone sang of the agonies of disillusionment and war she fought her own battle and won a modicum of relief from pain, the torment in her heart eased by the sublime beauty of the music. Oblivious to her surroundings, she lay stretched out in a lounger beside the pool while the long hot day drew to an end in the freshening coolness of twilight.

The sun had set and the first stars of the evening were glittering in the green sky when the church bells sounded and the unaccompanied chorus sang the final cadence. As the voices rolled out in the beautiful Latin words, '*Requiescant in pace. Amen,*' Lorena drew a deep breath, opened her eyes, and froze.

Beside her, only feet away, Bourne leaned against a pillar which held up the terrace pergola, his expression as absorbed as that on her own face, his eyes fixed on the topmost branches of the pohutukawa tree, crimson with the mass of its flowers against the pallor of the sky. He turned, asking derisively, 'Is that your sort of music?'

'Yes.' She swung her feet on to the flagstones, stood up prior to going. 'I'm sorry,' she began defensively, 'that I used it—I thought——'

'—that I was safely immersed in the beach house?' His smile was without humour. 'I'm sorry to spoil your orgy of emotion.'

'What do you mean?'

It took only a few steps for him to be in front of her. One hand snaked out to touch the stains of the tears she had wept for him. 'Does Britten always affect you so strongly that you cry when you hear him?' he asked softly, his eyes gleaming with some unknown emotion.

Lorena's heart seemed to block in her throat. It was almost as though he knew who those tears had been for.

Conscious of the betraying pulse which beat like a feather in her throat, she said huskily, 'That—the War Requiem—yes. It's so sad.'

Sad was an inadequate word to express the music's effect on her, but she could not think straight with him so close.

'You look like a forlorn nymph,' he said deep in his throat, while his glance slid from her face to her bare shoulders and thence to the softly rounded curves of her breasts.

Lorena heard the sharp, indrawn breath, looked up to see his mouth compress into that mixture of ruthlessness and desire which she had seen before, and said swiftly but unevenly,

'Well, I'm not a forlorn nymph, or anything so poetic, so you can stop pretending to be a satyr.'

'Is that how you see me?' The question came softly, his lips barely moving as he said the words, his whole expression predatory as a bird of prey intent upon its victim.

Lorena flinched as his hand moved from the stains on her cheeks to her throat, clasping it loosely yet with latent strength. She could see a muscle moving above the hard line of his jaw, caught the faint male fragrance and felt desire which was sharper than any pain.

Before it could render her helpless to the hypnotic spell he was casting over her she said recklessly,

'Hardly, but you must admit you do tend to lie in wait.'

It seemed that he hadn't heard her, for he smiled, but she saw turbulence deep within the darkness of his eyes and her gaze, proud and hard, fell as a great wash of colour crimsoned her cheeks. A shiver touched her skin with cold; she bit her lip, afraid as she had never been before in the presence of a man.

'Bourne——' she whispered, and tried to step away from him.

That smile grew, and with it the violence that was implicit in his hand at her throat. Lorena felt it leashed, looked up to see his intention in the demonic purposefulness of his features, then the cruel urgency of his mouth on hers blocked out her protest, even as his hands swept her into such close proximity that she felt as though they were lovers, naked together in the urgency of their passion, for the warmth of his body rendered the damp flimsiness of her bikini a negligible protection.

His mouth hurt, pressing her lips open as though he wanted to punish her. Lorena tensed herself to resist him, hating the lust she felt in his plundering of her mouth against her will.

Then, moving with a swiftness which shocked her, he lifted her from her feet and carried her across to the little summerhouse, his mouth still on hers but tenderness replacing the anger and contempt which had made that first onslaught so humiliating.

And Lorena was lost, her body and heart responding to his practised seduction of her senses. When he set her down on the chaise-longue she sighed, accepting his caresses and the wild sweet clamour of her nerves with no further demur, her whole being drowned in an ecstasy she had never known could exist. Winding her arms around his shoulders, she drew him down beside her, offering the taut slenderness of her body to his passion.

His hands at her breasts were gentle but tantalising, his mouth soft and compelling so that Lorena tensed with need, revelling in the hardness of his strength against her, and her own wholehearted response to it.

And then he said quite coolly against her mouth, 'A not unwilling nymph, indeed. I know of a more comfortable bed than this one, honey. Why not come there with me? At least we won't have to worry about the Robinsons breaking in on us.'

His words were like a bucket of cold water. With a soft bitter cry she pushed his hands away from her, sitting up in a movement so swift it took him by surprise. He lay quite still, his expression as coldly analytical as that of a mathematician gazing at an equation, while Lorena fumbled to cover her breasts with the inadequate bikini top.

Shame washed over her in a great sheet of crimson as he watched, seemingly unmoved by her proximity, his eyes hooded and implacable.

'No, thanks,' she said stiffly, discovering that her tongue, like her fingers, seemed to be tied in knots.

He stood up, towering over the lounger. 'You're quite a tease,' he observed dispassionately. 'Just how far would you have let me go? Complete seduction, and then squalled rape? It can be quite a profitable ploy, but believe me, honey, you picked the wrong man.'

'Stop it,' she whispered, managing at last to cover herself. With tears pricking her eyes and a hard lump at the back of her throat she continued, 'I had no intention——'

'Oh, don't take me for a fool,' he interrupted harshly, a white line around his mouth. 'You've had me wondering about your game ever since you got here. Advance—then retreat, and all the time that air of untouched sweetness. Just what do you want of me, Lorena Tanner?'

Angry in her turn, she swung herself off the chaise-longue, her expression scornful as the sparkle in her golden eyes. 'I don't want anything of you,' she retorted, defiance raising her voice above its normal pitch. 'It's what you want of me that's more to the point. Why don't you leave me alone?'

'Because you don't want me to.'

Her angry denial was brushed aside as if she hadn't spoken. 'No, admit that, at least! You want me, but you're not prepared to face it. You'll allow yourself to be seduced, but you haven't got the courage to give yourself freely. Well, I'm not prepared to be satyr to your nymph. I want you, but all my love affairs have been conducted on terms of equality, with no exploitation. If you're not prepared to face facts freely and openly, I can do without you.'

Lorena bit her lip, her mind rejecting the realisation that he had a little right on his side. Had he continued to make love to her she would have surrendered to him, only counting the cost afterwards when her passion had ebbed, but she could not—however much she loved him—submit to him in cold blood. It was against every principle, every ideal she possessed.

One glance at the flat, contemptuous countenance he presented to her showed her that any attempt to explain her attitudes would fail.

But she had to try. 'At least give me credit for not squalling rape,' she said numbly, looking about for her wrap.

'I don't know.' The words were almost expressionless, only the fires still burning deep within the depths of his eyes revealing the banked emotions he had so carefully in control.

Those eyes narrowed, became cruelly stabbing as he went on conversationally, 'I don't know whether that virginal air is real, or just clever fakery. When it comes down to the real nitty-gritty, Lorena Tanner, I don't know much about you.'

Feeling as though he had cut her heart out, she flashed, 'I'd have thought that your experience would have told you instantly. You've had so much, from what you've said.'

'Jealousy?'

Realising what a trap she had fallen into, how close she had come to revealing the extent of her feelings for him, she called on every ounce of pride she possessed. 'Jealousy? Hardly. I'd have to love you for that—and I don't. I'm just thankful that I don't treat making love as a game, a pastime, as you seem to. I don't want you.'

'You're lying.' Bourne smiled with sardonic lack of humour and ran his hand slowly along the line of her shoulders, stopping at the nape of her neck. 'You're trembling,' he said softly. 'You're not afraid of me, and you're not cold, so that leaves only one thing. This.'

Lorena drowned in the sweetness of his kiss, felt her self-control and sanity slip again before, with a muffled cry, she tore herself away from him, her eyes bruised and angry, her mouth a scarlet mark of shame in the pallor of her face.

'Will you *leave* me *alone*!' she hissed, furious with herself, even more angry with him for making such a fool of her.

'Oh, sure, honey,' he drawled cynically. 'Just stay out of my way, will you, in case my overweening lust gets the better of me.' He got up, turned to go out into the darkness, then said over his shoulder, 'Your wrap is at the end of the lounger by the pool, if that's what you were looking for.'

Lights flowered inside the house. He had gone into the big living room. As Lorena made her way along the terrace, the stones still warm from the day's sun, she saw him at the bar mixing himself a drink.

No doubt to drown his disappointment at not

finding her complaisant enough to spend the night with him she thought, horrified at her own cynicism.

A long time later, after she had showered every trace of his touch from her body, she pulled on a sprigged cotton brunch coat and sat in the cane chair at the foot of her bed, gazing unseeingly through the screen doors at the soft evening outside.

It was very still, very quiet, apart from the distant call of a morepork from the Haworths' bush and the low murmur of the television set along in Peggy's sitting room. Still cool enough in the evenings to require a wrapper, it was pleasant after the heat of the day to be able to feel the caress of the air on her damp skin. This first month of summer was often the loveliest of the season, she mused. January's weather was frequently hot and windy, and in February the heat could be stifling, rendering nights uncomfortable and the days so enervating that tempers were in a state of constant irritation.

Too, in December there was Christmas to look forward to. Very deliberately Lorena recalled past Christmases, when her parents had conspired to produce such excitement and happiness that it seemed impossible she had ever been so carefree. Even these past two years Peggy and Sel had taken the place of the family she had lost; she had gifts for them carefully wrapped in her drawer, and they would have bought a small gift to present to her before breakfast on Christmas Day.

This year would be different. Restlessly she got to her feet and began to pace the floor, her expression bleak as she tried to settle the turmoil in her mind and heart. With an effort at logic she endeavoured to sort and arrange her emotions, only to have to admit that she could not separate emotion from need. And all, emotions, desires, principles, paled in the revelation of her love.

Slowly, as the soft summer night wore on, she began to see that it was the very fact of this love which prevented her from becoming his mistress. If she loved him less there would be less danger in knowing him as a lover, but because she had lost her heart to him she knew that there could be no more than temporary pleasure and ease in the warmth of his arms.

She loved, and because of that she could be content with nothing less than a like love from him.

A bitter smile touched her lips. If that last interlude had shown her nothing else she had been made very aware of his attitude towards love. Direct, straightforward and without exploitation—a kind of swapping of sensual pleasure for as long as it took one or both of the partners to become sated. After that, no doubt, a businesslike farewell and the cheerful thought that they were still friends.

The fool! Did he really think that things were that simple? Lorena had to admit her total lack of knowledge of the world he inhabited, but she was a student of human nature and she was prepared to bet her new Italian shoes that very few women could be as practical and ruthless about passion as that.

Few men, too, surely. Unless at some time they had made a conscious decision not to allow themselves the luxury of emotion in their affairs. And that, she was almost certain, would mean a severe blow to self-esteem some time in the past.

It was an intriguing thought, one which took her mind from the ache in her breast. Like a vivid ghost Bourne's face sprang to mind, brooding, sensual, the light of mockery never far from the dark eyes, suberbly handsome; and emanating from him that something which set him apart, an authority rooted in character. She could not imagine any woman who would not feel a quickened heartbeat in his presence, but that, she thought wryly, was the purely physical aspect of it, the kind of basic chemistry which called female to male, weakness to strength.

Any woman who loved him would have to transcend that, accept him as he was, moody, bad-tempered in many ways, driven by a need she could not understand to express himself in his music.

And she did. Just as simply as that. If he asked her for a commitment she would make it joyfully, gladly, not counting the cost. But she would not permit him to give her only part of himself, and that part perhaps the least important. Even as she realised that, her breath came faster through her lips at the thought of his lips on hers, and she knew that she was fooling herself if she thought that any physical relationship between them could be construed unimportant.

Of course sex was important! But as a joyful affirmation of love, not a slaking of desire with nothing beyond it but that.

The television had long been silent when she sat down again, looking at her tensely clasped hands. Luminous figures on her watch showed her that it was well after midnight. Fortunately she had not turned the light on; Peggy might have come along to see what was the trouble had she noticed a light.

Impulsively she rose and pushed back the screen doors, walking out on to her tiny balcony to lift her face to the sky. Yes, there they were, her old friends, their majestic procession across the blue-black firmament always a rebuke to the puny woes of humanity. A meteor fell, two more streaked in fiery destruction, and then all was still again. Lorena felt awe, and pain and a great emptiness, and with the tears came a release of all of the emotions she had held in such close check, so that when she finally climbed into bed she fell instantly to sleep.

Some demon of creation seemed to have Bourne in its thrall once more. He began to spend most of his time down at the beach house, occasionally even sleeping there.

Peggy tutted and sent baskets of food down, but with growing anxiety Lorena noticed that little of her delicious cooking was being eaten. Once she remonstrated with him and was curtly put in her place.

'When I want someone to fuss over me I'll send for my mother,' he said harshly.

Not intimidated, Lorena snapped back, 'Very well, just keep on upsetting Peggy by turning down her cooking!'

He looked sharply at her, then rubbed a hand across his forehead before stretching. 'O.K., O.K., I'll eat—for Peggy. Come for a swim with me.'

'Is that an order?'

'Yes, damn you, it is!' The explosion seemed to have left him without resources, for he turned and blundered into the sofa, straightened up and stood staring at it as if it had lain in wait for him.

Lorena hid her concern with a smile. 'You need sleep, not exercise.'

'I'll sleep if you'll come with me.'

'Sleeping, or swimming?'

As soon as she had said it she knew that she had made a mistake and cursed her loose tongue. He turned, that slow smile she distrusted touching his lips, his expression at once alert and interested.

'Changed your mind?'

'No,' she said promptly, prepared for instant flight if he should come any closer, every nerve prickling with the excitement his presence roused in her.

'But you can't resist being provocative.'

She shrugged, aware of the justice of this. Bourne was too perceptive not to appreciate her dilemma, and apparently not chivalrous enough to refuse to press his advantage.

'Why, Lorena? Why back off, yet refuse to let go?'

A flush touched her cheeks at the derisive tone of his voice, but she lifted her head and answered proudly, 'Call it bloody-mindedness if you like, I'm sorry. I'll watch my tongue in future.'

'It might be a good idea,' he said softly, watching her as though he had her under a microscope. 'God knows why I don't seduce you and have it done with. We'd both be a lot happier. I must have a strong streak of chivalry in me somewhere.' His voice altered, became rough with tension. 'Move, will you! Tell Peggy I'll eat her contributions. And just to allay your tender concern, I'll sleep.'

Lorena fled, feeling that she had made rather a fool of herself.

That afternoon they all drove in to Paihia for a final shopping burst before Christmas. It was hot and sticky and very crowded with tourists and those who owned cottages and houses in the Bay. Lorena helped Peggy in the grocery store, then left her to watch the tourists as they came and went at the centre by the jetty. They interested her immensely, these family parties as most of them were, the children high-spirited and sunburned, the women usually somewhat harassed, the men with their variety of hats to keep the sun from city-pale noses.

Bi-coloured towelling efforts with a brim all around were fashionable this year, Lorena noted, and among the women, sun-frocks, really only appealing on the young. Among adolescents the fashion for tight jeans was still in full swing with little almost-nothing halter-necked suntops. Lorena grinned, thinking that she, in her wrap-around skirt and cool cotton blouse, had no place in the fashion stakes but was probably the coolest there. Impecunious university students couldn't change their styles according to the dictates of fashion, which explained why many of them looked a little old-fashioned.

The sun beat down on her bare arms and head, drugging her into a state almost like sleep. From the end of the jetty the turquoise and white ferries disgorged their passengers before taking on another load. A big tourist bus swept into the car-park, stopped and let off a swarm of middle-aged women before moving out again. As he went past the driver winked at Lorena. She grinned back.

Small boats buzzed back and forth, tiny yachts erratically sailed by small children miraculously avoided hitting each other, and adolescent girls paraded up and down the jetty, wriggling their neat, pert rears as they giggled and scanned the crowds eagerly.

Lorena sighed, envying them their freedom from care and heartache. And because the thought of her hopeless love tended to make her too dewy around the eyes she took sunglasses from her bag and slipped them on, cursing Bourne for coming between her and her simplest pleasures.

The dark glasses made looking out to sea much easier. Across the Russell side of the bay, between the two small islands which acted as sentinels for the channel into the Paihia jetty, a huge yacht swung slowly at anchor. Lorena wished she had binoculars, for this vessel was so big it seemed incredible that it should be privately owned. Perhaps it was one of the big charter yachts from overseas on a Pacific cruise. Accustomed as she was to the small thirty- or forty-foot yachts owned by most New Zealanders, she estimated this one to be in the region of a hundred feet. A real ocean-goer, she thought, screwing up her eyes as she tried to pick up the flag. It was too far away, however.

A movement beside her heralded Sel. Lorena smiled at him and together they watched the passing throngs in companionable silence. Lorena was unaware of the contrast they made, Sel, compact, weatherbeaten and tough, she as tall as he, a cool vision of loveliness made mysterious by the dark glasses which hid her eyes.

She pointed out the yacht. 'It must be almost as big as the *Spirit of Adventure*,' she said, referring to the lovely ship which a businessman's philanthropy had bestowed on the youth of New Zealand. The *Spirit* was a familiar and lovely sight in the Bay, always there with a youthful crew for Waitangi Day in February when the country celebrated the signing of the Treaty of that name which had set the pattern for subsequent dealings between Maori and Pakeha, as the Maoris called the Europeans who had found their lovely, savage land.

'Hardly,' Sel snorted, 'but she's a big one. Ah well, we'll be calling into Russell on the way home to pick up some things, so we'll get a closer look at her.'

Russell was only a little less busy than Paihia. Here most of the people thronging the waterfront road were from the yachts in the bay. Sel and Lorena wandered down the jetty admiring and criticising with the carefree attitude of people who know they will never be in the position to choose something as expensive as any of the sleek yachts or launches tied to the jetty or at anchor in the bay.

'There she is,' Sel motioned towards the beautiful black schooner in the bay. 'Dwarfs most of these, doesn't she?'

'Where's she from? Your distance sight is better than mine. Can you read those words on her stern?'

'Yes, *Demon* from Balboa, U.S.A. Wonder where Balboa is?'

Even afterwards Lorena could only think that whatever angel had charge of coincidences must have really enjoyed himself.

For a diffident voice from behind asked in a very broad American accent, 'Excuse me, sir, but you have been pointed out to me as the man in charge of a place called Waiwhetu.' He read the name from a piece of paper in his hand, frowning in case he mispronounced it.

Sel nodded, his expression wary as he took in the immaculate white uniform on the tall, middle-aged man facing him.

'Yes, that's so.'

'I'm from *Demon* out there in the bay. We have a passenger for Waiwhetu.'

Sel frowned. 'We've heard nothing about a guest

arriving now. Normally Mr Read's office lets us know.'

The American drawl sharpened slightly. 'Miss Johnson has been invited by your present guest, Mr Kerwood.'

CHAPTER SEVEN

SUBCONSCIOUSLY Lorena had known, had felt that something must happen to break the deadlock which existed between them, but she felt her cheeks pale at the implications behind the man's statement. Desolation so intense that it was like a pit beneath her feet made her bite her lip as she half-turned away, thankful that she still wore sunglasses to shield her expression.

'I see.' Sel spoke slowly, weighing up the situation. Then he said, 'I'll just ring from the store. Give me five minutes. Lorena, go and find Peg, will you?'

Conscious of the swift glance that the American sailor sent her, Lorena nodded and trailed back to the shore.

'Here's a fine thing,' Sel muttered. 'I'll bet he's done no such thing. He'd have let us know.'

Privately Lorena agreed with him, but some perverse spirit goaded her into saying, 'He might not have thought it important. He knows by now that Peggy can cope with anything.'

'She likes courtesy, and he's been fair enough until now.'

Sel disappeared into the store while Lorena ran Peggy to earth talking to a friend outside the pleasant museum where the small replica of Captain Cook's *Endeavour* was the prize exhibit.

As soon as she saw Lorena she said her goodbyes

and moved purposefully towards the girl, asking, 'Is Sel ready to go?'

As quickly as she could Lorena acquainted her with the latest developments, hoping that the odd wobble in her voice would be attributed to her hurry.

'It doesn't sound like Bourne,' Peggy commented when she had finished. 'Still, we've enough food to feed an army. Do you think whoever else is on the yacht will expect to stay too?'

'I don't know.' Lorena thought, then said, 'The chap said "a passenger for Waiwhetu". It doesn't sound like it, does it?'

'No. Still, they have different ways of saying things. Is that the yacht?'

Demon lay, apparently deserted, in the bay, dwarfing all the boats around her. She looked opulent, a visitor from a wider, richer world.

Shortly, Lorena answered, 'Yes.'

Sel was waiting for them, his expression carefully blank. 'It's O.K.,' he said, as they came up. 'He seemed quite happy to have her, although I'll swear he didn't know about her arrival. You wait here and I'll arrange things with *Demon*.'

Miserably conscious that the day was hot, that she was tired and hungry, that Miss Johnson would be beautiful in that glossy American way, Lorena stood beside Peggy, her unseeing eyes focussed on the rusty red carpet of fallen flowers at the foot of the pohutukawa trees which shaded the street.

After a moment Peggy said abruptly, 'You'll get over it, you know.'

Startled, Lorena looked up, met the older woman's compassionate glance, and could not prevent the wave of colour which washed over the smooth tanned skin beneath her sunglasses. Subduing an absurd desire to cry on Peggy's shoulder, she swallowed before answering in a voice almost too low to hear, 'I know. Don't worry about me.'

'I don't,' Peggy told her, looking straight ahead as if such an intimate conversation embarrassed her. 'You've got plenty of pride, not like some I know. And dignity. That helps.'

Sel came back, frowning but not altogether displeased. 'You drive home, Peg. I'll pilot them around to Waiwhetu. She's apparently got a mountain of luggage and she doesn't want publicity!'

Both he and Peggy delivered themselves of a sound which could be described as a snort, then he was gone and Peggy was saying comfortably, 'You can drive, Lorena. I don't like taking the car down that narrow road in summer with all the tourists about.'

It was kindly done, and it worked, for Lorena concentrated fiercely all the way back and had no time to spend on the aching organ which was her heart. Once back she found herself putting away vast quantities of groceries while Peggy made up the bed in the room she assigned to this Miss Johnson.

'Get some flowers ready, will you, there's a dear,' she said, reappearing. 'Use some of those green and cream zinnias. They'll blend in beautifully.'

The green bedroom was at the far end of the corridor from Bourne's; Lorena thought bleakly that a few feet of hallway wasn't likely to make much of a chaperone! But she arranged the zinnias carefully and took them along, to find Peggy dusting the already immaculate furniture.

'Soap,' she muttered, 'tissues, perfume—yes, that's

O.K. Lorena, get out the cream set of towels, will you? And the biscuits from the pantry, though if she's a typical American she'll live on salads. And some magazines in case she reads in bed.'

Thank God Bourne was nowhere in evidence, Lorena told herself with dull resignation. He hadn't even appeared by the time the yacht's anchor chain rattled into the clear waters of Waiwhetu bay. Peggy and Lorena were indulging in a snatched cup of tea; they looked at each other with some concern, then Peggy said, 'Sel will bring her up. Finish your tea.'

Peggy went out to meet Miss Johnson, ordering a by now jittery Lorena to stay in the kitchen and prepare the cold soup for dinner.

She came back looking stunned. 'Miss Johnson! It may be her real name, of course, but she's Ginny Hopkins. And some woman, if first impressions are at all reliable.'

Lorena felt as though Peggy had hit her over the heart. Dismay, she discovered, made you go cold all over, dimmed the sun through the window, sent the blood whirling hideously through your head. Ginny Hopkins was a film star, a beautiful raven-haired slip of a thing in the most modern of idioms, already renowned for her unconventional way of life and a string of brilliant films.

Perhaps it was at that moment that Lorena abandoned any faint hopes she still nursed of Bourne's falling in love with her. Like all relinquishment of hope it was a painful, almost shattering experience, but she was not given any time to brood or indulge in self-pity, for Peggy said briskly:

'You keep going with that meal, will you. I'll go and unpack her things.'

'Of course!'

Peggy was already half way out of the door. Lorena, warmed by the older woman's concern for her feelings, glanced at her watch and set to with a will. At least, she thought, as she put the cucumber soup into the refrigerator, at least she wouldn't have to suffer Bourne's presence at the dinner table any longer. The fascinating Ginny Hopkins would take up all of his time.

They dined out on the terrace; there was no sign of anyone about when Lorena set the table there, so she could only deduce that they were together in the beach house. Much later, when she and Peggy had done the dishes, she heard the stereo playing a series of slow ballads, perfect for setting a mood of sensual abandon, and to drive away the torture this aroused in her decided to expend her energy in swimming.

But not in the pool, and certainly not from Waiwhetu Beach itself, which left only the cove. For a moment she hesitated, then set her jaw in a typically resolute fashion. Bourne would be too busy to care where or when she swam.

The water was as warm as milk, but the sky threatened a break in the weather; high clouds like the scales of a fish were touched with gold and tangerine. The light breeze was coming in from the north, so within a few days there would be rain from that quarter. Lorena swam until she was exhausted, then sat on the rocks and dried herself, watching wistfully as the last of the pleasure craft made their way to anchorage. If she could only go now before her stupid love brought her any more pain—but she could not leave Peggy, and she would not give Bourne Kerwood the satisfaction of knowing just how strongly his girl-friend's arrival affected her. Pride was probably a sin, but at the moment she felt that it was the only thing which was able to put much-needed stiffening in her backbone.

'Oy! Mermaid!'

Gordon's voice broke into her reverie; half-started, she looked around, to discern the two boys in the Haworths' runabout, about fifty yards away.

'Want some hapuka?' he called out now.

'Lovely! Did you catch it?'

'Yes. We're on our way back in. Like to swim out and get it?'

She smiled. 'O.K.'

Because of the rocks which sheltered it the cove was a little difficult to bring a runabout into, so Lorena didn't blame Gordon for asking her to swim. Leaving her towel on a rock she made a neat dive into the water and swam out through the rapidly falling twilight to where Gordon was busy tying up a splendid groper in a plastic bag.

'There you are,' he said, leaning over the side to give it to her. 'Cleaned and all. Sel will have to cut it into steaks, but it couldn't be fresher. Don't drop it.'

'I won't.'

Mark grinned and called out, 'Be careful of the octopus.'

'What octopus?'

'Bless my soul, *any* octopus!'

Whereupon both boys roared with smug laughter as the runabout headed off around the point.

Within a few seconds Lorena was back at her towel, only to find it occupied, or presided over, by a distinctly unfriendly Bourne. Her heart gave a couple of erratic thumps as she remembered the first night she had been at Waiwhetu. He had met her at almost the same place, demanding that she leave the cove to him. Had she known then just how powerfully he was going to affect her she would have done better to pack up her bags and go altogether, she thought wearily, bracing herself for another outburst.

Instead he said smoothly, 'What have you got there?'

She told him, accepting the towel when he handed it to her, glad of its size. It covered her completely except for the slim tanned length of her legs.

'You don't have to use the fish as armour,' he told her, removing the plastic bag from her grasp with a smile she could discern as amused. 'I'm not going to hit you.'

Some of the tension seeped from her. 'I didn't think you were.'

'No? It must have been something else you were afraid of then,' he rejoined, moving up beside her as she made her way over the rocks. 'Have you been hiding?'

Such a direct attack threw her off balance for a moment, but she made a gallant recovery. 'No. Why should I hide?'

'Far be it from me to try to fathom out the workings of your mind.'

Thankful that he didn't follow up her foolhardy attempt to carry the war into the enemy's country, she said crisply,

'Has Miss Hopkins settled in?'

'Ginny? Oh yes, very well. She likes the place.'

'Most people do.'

He laughed. 'Don't bristle at me. Ginny's a little

spoilt when it comes to beauty spots, but even she admits this has something special.'

Determined not to ask just how long the glamorous Ginny was staying, Lorena kept her tongue clamped tightly between her teeth; so resolved was she not to say anything that his hand on her arm made her start with something like fear.

'What the hell?' His grip tightened, forcing her to stop.

By now they had climbed halfway up the path to the cliff top, but in spite of the narrowness he swung her to face him.

In the darkness of the pohutukawa trees he was barely discernible, but although she couldn't see his face Lorena could feel the anger which held him in grip.

'You don't have to flinch away from me as if I were poison,' he muttered. 'What do you think I am—a rapist?'

Unbearably affected by his closeness, she swallowed, her throat too dry to make the attempt to talk. After a moment she managed, 'Of course not! You—you surprised me. I wasn't expecting you.'

It was a lame reason, even though it happened to be the truth, so she was not surprised when he said savagely, 'You're as taut as piano wires. What the hell is the matter with you?'

'Nothing.'

'Oh, for God's sake!' He almost flung her from him.

Lorena stumbled, put out her hand for support and fell, twisting her ankle. Her breath hissed through her lips as she stood up again, determined not to let him see that she was in pain. With lips pressed tightly together she pulled herself up against a big bough, holding on to it a moment before testing her weight on the sore ankle.

Fortunately it wasn't too bad. She managed a step.

'You're limping,' Bourne stated on a note of accusation.

'It's nothing.'

'I don't enjoy hurting you,' he declared curtly, scooping her up with ease. 'Carry the fish, will you?'

Lorena felt an unbearable desire to relax in his grip, knew that she must resist this weakness and said with as much stiffness as she could infuse into her voice, 'I'm too heavy——'

'Just shut up!'

And such was the savagery in his tones that she subsided.

In spite of his strength he was sweating when they reached the top of the cliff, and had to set her on her feet, holding her steady with an arm around her shoulders.

Against her will Lorena looked up. Though the rapid twilight had fallen her eyes were accustomed to the starlight and she could make out his features, the clear, strong lines of the bones which would make him just as handsome in old age as he was now, the frown which marred his forehead, the controlled sensuality of his mouth. She felt her heart contract with the desire to smooth away the lines, to ease the tension she could discern in his expression.

He must have heard the soft sigh which was the only sign of her feelings, for he said quietly, 'Oh, Lorena——'

'Bourne! Bourne, honey, where are you?'

Ginny Hopkins' voice was the opposite of strident, but to Lorena it sounded like a fire siren through the quiet garden, reminding her of what his nearness had managed to temporarily obliterate from her memory.

With a swift movement she pulled away, the set of her shoulders very straight as she said, 'See, the ankle is perfectly all right now.'

'Lorena!'

Anger and humiliation chilled her tones to ice.

'Miss Hopkins is calling you,' she said stonily as she turned away towards the kitchen entrance.

Normally he moved as silently as a cat, so it was odd that she should hear him as he walked across the grass to where Ginny Hopkins waited. Or perhaps, Lorena thought, love sharpened the ears as well as making the other senses more acute. Whatever, after a few seconds she heard their voices in conversation.

Pride, she discovered, might stiffen the backbone, but it didn't do anything for the kind of desolation heartbreak brings. It would have been easier if she had been able to hate the beautiful girl who seemed on such intimate terms with Bourne, but subsequent days proved that, film star or no film star, Ginny Hopkins was warm and friendly, those glorious green-blue eyes clear and guileless as the summer sky. Against her will Lorena felt her mask of reserve slipping at the other girl's open invitation to friendship.

'You're a stunning thing,' she said suddenly one day. Lorena was cleaning silver under the jacaranda tree with the cat draped over her ankles and bees humming purposefully in the garden behind her. It was very pleasant, if one could ignore the permanent ache in her heart; Lorena felt herself tighten defensively as Ginny strolled across the lawn, and consciously willed every muscle to relax. It would not take much for Ginny to realise that Lorena viewed her with mixed emotions; those eyes might be guileless, but the brain behind them was astute.

At that surprise opening remark she felt some embarrassment. Accustomed as she was by now to American frankness, it still had the power to startle her.

'Thank you,' she replied demurely, wishing that she was as stunningly beautiful as this woman.

'I mean it!' Ginny dropped down on to the rug, pushing the cat away. 'No, you're too heavy, and too hot, you gorgeous beast. You look surprised, Lorena. I'm sure Bourne hasn't spent all of this time here without telling you how lovely you are. He has an eye for feminine beauty.'

The soft tones held a low, teasing note, as if Ginny was inviting her to join in a joke.

Lorena swallowed, and said wryly, 'I don't think he's called me lovely. Just about everything else, though. I annoy him immensely.'

Laughter warmed the sea-blue eyes which were fixed so steadily on Lorena's face as if seeking to read every nuance of expression.

'Do you fight?' Ginny chuckled. 'Poor Bourne! He wouldn't be used to that. Mostly girls just fall at his feet and lie there gasping. What do you really think of him?'

Frankness was all very well, but surely even in the States one couldn't expect a stranger to be so candid after such short acquaintance!

'He's very attractive,' Lorena told her dryly, making a big thing of polishing the tines of a fork.

'Is that all?'

The older girl's voice still had that subtle, teasing, coaxing note; her smile created an intimacy which did not exist between them. Lorena felt as though her privacy was being invaded; as though Ginny intruded on a precious, almost sacred part of her being.

With acting ability she didn't know she possessed, she answered briskly, 'Come now, Miss Hopkins, what do you expect me to say? I've told you I find him attractive. I could give you a character reading, if you like, but you know him much better than I do.'

Not at all put out, the film star chuckled, stretching like a sleek kitten in the sun. 'The air here is like wine,' she said. 'And call me Ginny, will you? Miss Hopkins sounds like work—that's what they call me when they want me on the set. So Bourne snaps at you, does he? Normally he's very courteous—crushingly so, on occasion.'

'I know.' Forgetting the aloofness of a moment ago Lorena spoke with emphasis.

Came another delicious chuckle and then King barked and Gordon and Mark, arguing amiably, strolled through the narrow gap between the borders, both clad in swim trunks and nothing else, their torsos burnt brown by the sun.

'Who are these?' asked Ginny.

Lorena selected another fork. 'Neighbours,' she answered, smiling up at the boys as she introduced them to her beautiful companion.

Mark said eagerly, '*The* Ginny Hopkins in *The Clouds of Space*?' and when she nodded, obviously amused by his eagerness, demanded, 'Miss Hopkins, can you tell me how they did that bit when the sky exploded, and you and the other guy were blown right through the cloud and into the other universe?'

'Oh—dear!' Ginny gave him a rueful smile. 'I'm sorry, Mark, but I'm not at liberty to say. To tell you the truth, I'm not sure I could tell you, anyway, it's very technical and complicated. We wore harnesses, of course, and I got severely bruised in all sorts of improbable places.'

Both boys laughed, put at their ease by her charm and the gaiety of her rueful smile, and as Lorena finished off the cutlery and began on napkin rings, they talked to her about various aspects of film-making, discussing the subject with a knowledge which astonished Lorena.

'We do it at school,' Gordon explained when Ginny commented on their breadth of knowledge. 'And I think TV makes you much more critical of films.'

'I think you're probably right.' Ginny picked up a napkin ring and began removing the dried polish, her slender fingers moving automatically. It was obviously something she had done frequently before, Lorena thought after her first shock had passed. And why not? Actors and actresses, film stars and pop singers were not a breed apart; their roots were in the same clay as the rest of humanity, even if their destiny took them to heights most people did not dream of.

Gordon broke a small silence by saying diffidently, 'We came to see if you'd like to go to the dig up at Rawle's Point, Lorena. Mark and I thought we'd take the runabout and go tomorrow. Didn't you say some of your friends were up there?'

'Yes. Yes, a couple at least.' Lorena frowned, thinking swiftly while Gordon told the interested

Ginny about the archaeological excavations undertaken by the University party each year.

Everything was ready for Christmas; she and Peggy had packed the freezer with already cooked supplies, the house was scoured from top to toe; Sel had even chosen a small tea-tree for a Christmas tree. Peggy would raise no objections to her going, and she had to confess that a day in the uncomplicated company of her two boy-friends would be a relief after the tension that emanated from Bourne.

'I'll just check with Peggy,' she said, getting to her feet.

Ginny grinned up at her. 'Do you think I'd be allowed along?' she asked demurely, casting a fleeting glance at Gordon, who blushed but said manfully:

'Of course, we'd be glad to take you, if you'd like to come.'

'Who's going where?' Bourne demanded from just behind Lorena, startling her into casting a hunted glance behind her. His dark eyes met hers with smooth amusement as he draped an arm across her shoulders, holding her with an impersonal strength which angered her as much as it excited her. Especially as she could feel Ginny's mocking, speculative gaze on her and cringed at the thought of just what was going through the other girl's mind.

Gordon explained, asking diffidently, 'Would you like to come too?'

There came an almost imperceptible increase in the pressure of his arm. 'Sure,' he drawled, 'it would make an interesting day's outing. Will Peggy let you off the leash, Lorena?'

'Yes, I think so,' she answered stiffly.

'Run off and ask her, there's a good girl, while we finish making arrangements.'

Seething at this summary dismissal, Lorena walked off with a back as stiff as a ramrod, heard Bourne's voice and the burst of laughter which followed it, and was betrayed into increasing her pace. He had no right to—to assume command so effortlessly, she told herself savagely.

It seemed that he had indeed assumed command, for when she appeared again with Peggy's permission it was to find the whole aspect of the proposed trip had changed. Instead of the Haworths' runabout they were to take Mr Read's big launch; as Lorena came up to the group she heard Bourne promise Ginny a moonlit trip home, and felt immediately a tide of desolation so strong that she almost blurted out a denial of Peggy's acquiescence.

But if she did that Bourne would know why. Pride held her erect as she nodded at Gordon's questioning glance. They looked like a tableau of summer, she thought, a group that a French Impressionist could have painted. Ginny leaned forward, her beautiful face alert and interested, those slender fingers still rubbing polish from the cutlery which winked and glittered in the dappled gold coins of the sunlight through the branches. The two boys lounged with the careless grace of youth, Bourne leaned against the smooth bole of the jacaranda, lithe and every bit as elegant as any Edwardian dandy in his casual clothes. The tree cast a deep pool of shade beyond which was the shimmering light of the sun and the vivid colours in Sel's borders, an incandescent blend of ripe golds and reds and purples against the hot, green foliage. Through the pohutukawas the sea burned, and above them the sky was a metallic blue sheen.

King lay against Bourne's feet, his long pink tongue hanging against his silvery-grey coat as he panted gently, while the cat had managed to snuggle against the soft curve of Ginny's knee and was lying on his back, paws waving gently as he dreamed.

Somebody laughed, Gordon moved aside to let Lorena sit down, and Peggy appeared with a tray bearing a huge frosted jug and glasses.

'Orange juice!' Mark exclaimed, leaping to his feet to help her. 'How did you know I was dying of thirst?'

Relinquishing the tray into his hands, Peggy permitted herself a smile. 'In this weather, young man, who wouldn't be? How about getting a couple of deck chairs, Gordon? Has anybody seen Sel?'

Bourne nodded. 'He's found another tree which he thinks is even better than the one we've already chosen for a Christmas tree. I think he wants us to go and have a look at it.'

'Oh——!' Gordon came hurtling back with the deck chairs in time to hear this. 'Gosh, Mark, you'd have let me forget, wouldn't you! Mrs Robinson, Mum wondered if we could cut fronds from your pongas to decorate the woolshed? For the dance.'

'One from each fern,' Peggy replied.

Ginny, who had laid down the polishing rag to accept a long glass of orange juice, looked startled. 'Tell me, what are pongas?' she asked, pronouncing the unfamiliar word with the ease of one whose ear for sounds has been refined by long training.

'Tree ferns,' Gordon pointed to a small clump just visible against the sea. 'See, those things with fronds like Catherine Wheels on top and a long black trunk. Miss Hopkins, they're one of New

Zealand's most potent symbols.' His voice rang with mock reverence. 'Our revered All Blacks wear the insignia of the silver fern when they go into battle.'

'O.K.,' Ginny retorted, grinning, 'who are the All Blacks?'

'Footballers.' Mark laughed outright at the expression on the actress's face, 'And not footballers as you know them, either. Rugby is a game for heroes!'

In the spirited exchange of conversation which followed on the respective merits of Rugby football as opposed to grid-iron, about which Ginny was surprisingly knowledgeable, Lorena felt an odd detachment. It was almost certainly her supersensitivity at the moment, but it seemed that she was very much on the periphery of the group, an onlooker gazing with big eyes at those more fortunate than her.

Unconsciously she looked up—saw Bourne smile, a swift cruelly derisive twist of his lips; Lorena looked away, the gold washed entirely from her eyes to leave them as green as the sea under a thunderstorm.

How could she love a man so much, yet hate and despise him too? she wondered wearily, oblivious of the boys as they leaped to their feet to show a laughing Ginny one of the finer points of their game with a cushion. If only he would leave her alone—but it seemed that the bond of the senses was almost as strong as the truer, more kindly ties of love. He wanted her, and because of that he could not forgive her for refusing him. Had there been anything of love in his feelings for her he would respect her wishes and not, she thought savagely, make casual love to her for lack of anything better to do, so that she was conscious of his presence every time he was anywhere near her.

She was being unfair; it was not his fault that her senses reverberated to his presence as if she were an instrument touched by a master hand, but it was only by whipping up her anger and pride that she could keep some self-respect intact.

The boys arrived back, drank more orange juice, teased Ginny with complete freedom from inhibitions, then drank yet more orange juice.

Peg lifted an eyebrow at the now empty jug.

'I'll get some more.' Lorena jumped to her feet, glad of an excuse to leave this altogether too carefree group.

In the kitchen it was cool and quiet, only the faint hum of the refrigerator breaking the silence. Working deftly Lorena sliced the oranges, squeezed the juice then tipped it into the jug, adding ice-cubes and water. The familiar task cooled her emotions, bringing a measure of tranquillity so it was doubly unfortunate that Bourne should have decided to follow her, the determination in his jaw making it clear that he intended to discuss something with her.

'What do you want?' she asked, not attempting to hide her hostility.'

'Don't tempt me,' he said softly, not smiling as colour rushed into her skin. Without giving her time to snap back an answer he went on in curiously flat tones, 'You'd better make sure that the Haworths invite Ginny to this woolshed dance of theirs.'

So that was it.

Lorena's heart felt as if it had reached the very nadir of hopelessness, but in a voice which matched his for impersonality replied, 'Of course they will!

The boys are probably asking her now, but you can be quite sure Mrs Haworth will ring up as soon as she hears that Miss Hopkins is here.'

'Good.' He lounged over to the sink, stared out of the window for a moment, then turned to survey her, thrusting his hands deep into the pockets of his jeans as he did so.

'Looking forward to tomorrow?'

She nodded, slicing another orange in half.

'Have you read the book Sel has about the dig?'

Surprised, she looked up, met the dark enigma of his glance and had to clear her throat before answering huskily, 'No. No, I haven't. I didn't know he had one.'

'He lent it to me a couple of days ago. I'll get it for you. It's really a tourist leaflet, so there's not much depth to it, but I found it interesting. I know very little about the pre-history of the Pacific.'

'Few people can claim to,' she answered, more at ease than she had been with him for a long time. 'It's a fascinating field of study.'

'More fascinating than I'd realised.' Without any comment he came across, lifted the tray and said quietly, 'I'm glad you like Ginny.'

Lorena felt her sinews stiffening, but said as calmly as she could manage, 'It would be hard not to, Bourne. She's an extremely charming person.'

'One of those rare people who have a simple, very direct appreciation of all of those things the rest of us get into tangles over,' he agreed smoothly. 'For Ginny everything is simple, she has an animal's attitude to life and living; it's to be enjoyed or endured.'

'She must be more complex than that,' Lorena objected, wondering what he was trying to tell her.

That they were lovers? Well, she had been almost certain of that, and anyway, what had their life to do with hers? she thought with sudden bitterness. They could flout conventions and because of their massive self-confidence, feel no remorse or self-doubt. But there was no easy way out for people like Lorena Tanner, who lived according to rules so deeply ingrained that even when caught in the grip of an emotion so strong that she was defenceless against it she could not give in to the promptings of her desire.

'You'll have to discover that for yourself,' he answered.

CHAPTER EIGHT

THE day dawned clear and cool with that breathless hush which was the promise of another lovely day. Lorena awoke heavy-eyed and tired, for she had found it difficult to sleep, caught in the coils of jealousy and bitterness which seemed her permanent bedfellows by now.

It had only been by the exercise of immense self-control that she had banished the evil mocking images her brain had conjured up in the scented darkness, visions of Bourne and Ginny locked in each other's arms, fantasies that tormented her until she had switched her light on and read determinedly. Even then, it had been well after midnight that she had felt calm enough in her mind to put out the light and relax on to the pillows. Fortunately sleep had followed soon after, but as she viewed her face in the bathroom mirror she could not help thinking that high cheekbones did little for one when one's eyes were shadowed and heavy-lidded with weariness.

Almost she decided to plead illness and stay at home; the prospect of a whole day spent watching Bourne and Ginny amuse themselves with each other could only strike chill into the depths of her heart. But Peggy would know why she stayed behind, and worse, she was almost certain that Bourne would, too.

So she packed a change of clothes, her swimsuit and towel and make-up kit into a bag, carefully placed sunglasses on top, before going out into the kitchen to begin preparing breakfast.

Peggy was already up. 'Good morning,' she said after one swift glance. 'I've got most of the stuff you'll need in these two coolers. Bourne said you'd be out until late, so I've put the wherewithal for dinner in the smaller one. Everything for lunch will be cold—jellied game, salads and iced soup. For dinner I've put in two steak pies, green salad and potato salad, and there's a bag of shelled peas to cook. For dessert there's peaches in Burgundy and ice cream for the boys, and a cheesecake just in case they need more.' She smiled, pointing to another container. 'And there are the snacks.'

Lorena managed an answering smile. 'I'll bet Mrs Haworth has packed as much.'

'Yes, and if I know those boys there'll be precious little left by the time you get home tonight. Well, that's that. Would you set the table? Bourne and Miss Hopkins are going to eat with us this morning. He wants to get away early.'

Somewhat to Lorena's surprise Ginny appeared at the table wide awake and cheerful, looking impossibly beautiful in a sun-frock which revealed the lovely lines of her body without unduly emphasising them.

As she ate her grapefruit Lorena thought wistfully that almost anyone would look dowdy beside such natural beauty, unaware that the contrast between the two of them seemed to enhance each girl's looks. The shadows in her gold-green eyes lent Lorena an air of mystery which was heightened by the set of her cheekbones and the controlled discipline of her mouth.

'More coffee?' When Bourne shook his head

Lorena got to her feet. 'Then if you'll excuse me ...'

'Where are you going?'

She lifted her brows as she turned to face him. 'There are a few things I'd like to do.'

He reacted to the note of defiance in her tones with an abrupt gesture, then seemed to think better of what he had intended to say. 'We'll be leaving in twenty minutes.'

'I'll be ready,' she returned, and left swiftly, before he could embarrass her any further. As she tidied and dusted the big living room she felt her anger seep away, leaving behind nothing but weariness which threatened to overwhelm her. But she was too vital for such a negation of emotion to last long. Life just wasn't *fair*, she thought with youth's passionate rebellion. To love without return seemed such a waste of emotion, such a waste of time and love and desire.

Unless there was something to be gained from it all. But what? Her love—and Bourne's swift response to her weakness—had certainly strengthened her will-power, she thought with cynical humour. Had she exercised a little less of that she would be his mistress by now. A touch of colour in her cheeks provoked her into telling herself fiercely that she was well out of that situation! Imagine just how shaming—how *humiliating*—to have given in to his experienced lovemaking and then for Ginny Hopkins to turn up!

Perhaps about the only thing she would gain from this whole mess was experience; experience which might stand her in good stead later on but which was painfully bought.

As she dusted the books she caught sight of a biography of Marian Anderson, the famous American contralto; it fell open at a photograph of the singer and Lorena stood for a long moment staring at the beautiful, serene face. There had been a woman who had fought and struggled for her art, who had treated every setback as a stepping stone towards her goal.

With the swift insight which was one of her strongest characteristics, Lorena realised that she had been wallowing in self-pity, allowing it to blind her to all that she had enjoyed in life, all that had given her strength.

Unconsciously, as she replaced the book, she squared her shoulders. So, she had fallen in love with Bourne, unwillingly and against her better judgment. And she had blamed him for her pain, as if he had set out to dazzle her into submission, as if she were too stupid, too ignorant to be able to see what was happening. Love came unbidden, came from within, it was not a spell cast by the beloved, but a response to something in him which she needed in spite of the cautionings of her brain.

Like a Victorian innocent she had behaved with a foolishness which made her cheeks hot with shame. How could she be so silly as to blame him for her emotions? With an honesty which was painful yet cleansing she forced herself to face the unpalatable facts, and with her honesty came release of a sort, so that she was able to admit to herself that he, at least, had been honest with himself and with her. It was she who had hidden behind a smokescreen of unstated provisos.

She had wanted him to love her, she had known that he could not, and she had refused to accept either friendship or a warmer relationship with him. He had called her a tease, and indeed, she thought sadly, her behaviour must have seemed very like that, at once advancing and retreating, responding to his ardour with eagerness yet refusing to accept anything more than kisses from him.

Well, it seemed that in Ginny he had both a friend and a lover; Lorena forced herself to accept that she had made a decision where he was concerned and she must now accept the consequences of that decision, however much it hurt. Perhaps that would be what she gained from this holiday, a little bit of self-knowledge, another step on the road to maturity.

And she could begin to show it by refusing to behave as if his presence was a challenge which brought out the very worst in her.

Which was all very well to decide in an empty room, not nearly so easy to carry out in the considerably more crowded confines of the launch when he seemed altogether too close and too—too *dear,* she owned hopelessly to herself. It was as if with her renunciation of any hopes for his love she discovered just how much she loved him, how very strongly the physical reality of the man affected her. Like the way he smiled at her, slow and secret, when Mark gave a yell of pure high spirits and chased Ginny down the wharf with a crab.

'She's not in the least frightened of crabs,' he murmured as he leaned over to pick up one of the coolers, 'but she's a real trouper and hates to disappoint an audience.'

The admiration in his voice hurt, but Lorena smiled back, and was rather pleased at the surprise she discovered in his eyes. 'She's very good with the boys,' she replied honestly. 'Some women would find them too boisterous.'

'She was a tomboy herself—grew up in the Rockies with a pack of brothers, so they'd be no novelty to her.'

Together they carried the bins of food into the small galley. Bourne set the two he carried on to the floor, asking, 'Are you going to leave them in these or use the refrigerator?'

'I'll put some of it in the fridge.' Bending, she took the lid from the one which held the dinner Peggy had packed.

'Lorena.'

She looked up, saw him stern and unsmiling. 'Yes?'

'Don't act the servant today, there's a good girl. Relax and enjoy yourself.'

Somewhat ashamed at her previous churlishness, she said, 'Well, I've never actually considered myself a *servant*, you know. But I promise not to rush around and wait on everyone.'

A wry smile tugged at the sensuous mouth while in his eyes there was appreciation not unmixed with mockery. 'O.K., that'll do for the present, honey. So unpack what's necessary and then get up on deck. I've a feeling you and I will be needed to add a note of sobriety to this party.'

And he could well be right, Lorena thought, for judging by the yells and thumps from above Ginny had reverted right back to her tomboy days.

But as the contents of the bin were loaded into the refrigerator the noise died down and before she had a chance to get up on deck the deep soft roar of the engine and the purposeful patter of feet from above warned that they were on their way.

For a moment Lorena hesitated, then set her shoulders and with chin tilted made her way through the cabin and out into the cockpit.

Perhaps it was her conscious resolution, perhaps the day and the company combined to make it flawless; whatever fortunate combination of circumstances were joined together they produced a time of enchantment. The boys were their amiable undemanding selves. Ginny someone who could become a dear friend, and Bourne—well, Bourne seemed to have shrugged off the black mood which had made him so caustic and today he was the companion she had always known he could be. And though he showed no preference for her company Lorena derived some comfort from the fact that he was no more friendly with Ginny than with her.

If that was pettiness, she thought, let it be! Just for today she was going to pretend that there was nothing but pure, uncomplicated friendship between them, no memories of passion, no anger and frustration and hurt. Just for today there would be no complications, even if her heart did beat double time every time he came into sight, and every nerve in her body felt his presence as though touched by him.

'You're very quiet—not feeling sick, are you?'

Mark's concerned question made her smile. 'Not in the least, just enjoying the scenery,' she fibbed.

'Mark's been telling us the names of all the islands.' That was Ginny, vital and vivid, her hair fluttering from beneath a bandeau, her slender form perfectly balanced on the dipping, swaying deck. 'Where exactly are we headed for, Mark?'

'Straight ahead, ma'am. See, there's a woolshed by the beach—that big red building. Well, beyond that row of trees is a nice secluded little bay, and that's where, a thousand or so years ago, a group of Maoris lived and died and ate gargantuan feasts of shellfish.'

'There's a good scallop bed just off the bay,' Gordon said from behind the wheel.

'Trust you to think of food,' said Mark loftily.

Bourne intervened from where he was keeping an unobtrusive eye on Gordon's steering, calling them to order.

'How many people go up each year to dig?' Ginny asked.

'About twenty or so.' Lorena felt Bourne's glance on her, smiled at him and went on, 'If I didn't have to work for my living I'd be there too.'

'*Work?*' Gordon hooted. 'You don't know the meaning of the word!'

'At least I don't eat my wages,' she retorted spiritedly.

Laughing, Gordon shook his fist at her. 'O.K., you win this time, but I'll get you yet.'

'How?'

He pretended to consider, then said slyly, 'I'll ask you for a dance—say, a waltz. I can't waltz,' he said to Ginny with a disarming air of innocence.

'Alas, my manners are impeccable,' Lorena said sadly. 'If he asks, I'll have to dance with him.'

'Did Mum ring you last night, Ginny?' Gordon had obviously just remembered.

'Yes, thank you. She sounds a sweetie, your mother, I told her I'd be honoured to come.'

'She's got some funny ideas,' Gordon said ingenuously. 'She thought she should come and ask you, but I told her she'd have to be pretty early up, because we're going out today and the dance is tomorrow night.'

Ginny's mouth twitched, but she replied solemnly

enough, 'Yes, she apologised for not bringing me the invitation in person, but explained that life is very informal around here. Which reminds me, Lorena; what shall I wear?'

'What you have on now would be fine,' Lorena told her.

Ginny grinned, casting a deprecatory glance at her bare shoulders. 'That informal, huh? Good, I'm looking forward to my first woolshed dance. Bourne, have you ever been to a woolshed dance?'

'Can't say that I have,' he said, moving away from Gordon to sit on the coaming next to Lorena. 'Barn dances, yes, but we don't have sheep where I come from.' He reached out and tucked a chestnut frond firmly behind Lorena's ear, his glance lazily amused yet guarded, as though challenging her to object.

Determined not to let him see how his most casual touch shook her, she smiled, saying lightly, 'Well, a barn dance and a woolshed dance would be much the same, I'd imagine. Who have you got to play, Gordon?'

'The Savage family. And records for the modern stuff.'

The rest of the voyage passed in a dreamy haze for Lorena. Bourne did not touch her again, but he did not move from her side, and although he addressed much of his conversation to Ginny, Lorena felt his closeness as if it were a magic cloak around her.

At last they arrived at the bay with the woolshed, tied up at the jetty there and walked along the well-marked track which led over a low rise to the bay where the university had its dig.

The sea danced and shimmered, the sun drew up the scents of the baked earth, sweet perfume of crushed grass, spicy crispness from huge old conifers sheltering the woolshed, the faint smell of sheep. On one of the hills a red tractor chugged peaceably towards a small knoll decorated with trees; from the bay ahead came a girl's laugh, and the sudden blare of a transistor, followed by a masculine bellow of 'Turn that thing down!'

When they reached the top of the rise they stopped by mutual, unspoken consent, to look down at the scene beneath. The tribe of Maoris had chosen their site with their customary skill, for their homes had been built on a small patch of slightly raised ground, above flood level and sheltered from the south by the rise. It was here that the main dig was situated, the ground marked off in plots like a chessboard, each one with one or two earnest sifters of soil squatting with noses close to the ground. A cluster of tents huddled around a marquee at the northern end of the bay across the small stream which wound its way over the flat.

'Interesting,' Ginny murmured. 'Let's go down.'

Their arrival was made easy by the fact that the first worker happened to be a girl Lorena knew quite well, both of them being keen members of the University Astronomy Club. Liz Stafford was in another hostel; they had talked idly of finding an apartment together.

'Hey!' she exclaimed, jumping to her feet. 'Hey, Lorena! Come to help?'

Lorena laughed. 'Sorry, no, Liz. This is Ginny and Bourne, Gordon and Mark. Folks, this is Liz, who stargazes with me when she has the time.'

If Liz was surprised at the very informal nature of the introduction she gave no indication of this, though her eyes widened slightly as they rested on Ginny, and even more when she saw Bourne.

'Nice to see you all,' she said cheerfully, placing her trowel carefully on the ground. One grubby forearm wiped her bangs away from her eyes. '*Do* say you want a conducted tour! I'm tuckered out, for all it's so early.'

Ginny responded immediately, her American accent lazy and warm on the ear. 'Of course we do. But if you're so hot now, how on earth do you manage in the afternoon?'

'Ah, we've adopted the delicious old habit of siesta. We sleep from one to four, and then work until quite late. The daylight saving is a blessing; we can keep going until nine at night. Come on and have a good look around.'

The day was almost enchanted, a time out of time, spent in the easy, informal atmosphere of the dig. Once Liz took the opportunity to mutter in Lorena's ears, 'Are they really who they look to be?'

'Yes, but they're not overly keen on any publicity.'

Liz grinned. 'I'll spread the word. You've got a lot of explaining to do when we get back, my girl.'

'I'll explain, I promise,' as Liz looked sceptically at her.

'You'd better,' was all that she said, but Lorena noticed the sideways glances cast by the other students as their visitors moved around. Ginny was interested, but Bourne revealed such knowledge of the technicalities that Professor Hamilton, a slender middle-aged woman whose family, fortunately, had inherited or acquired by osmosis her passion for archaeology, soon had him in tow, discussing the site with the gentle detachment she used with all of her colleagues.

Lorena could not help feeling an inordinate sense of pride; it helped to ease the pain of her love that he was intelligent as well as attractive. At least she hasn't lost her heart to sheer animal magnetism, she thought sardonically. Not always noted for their tolerence, these university students accepted Bourne as their equal in every way. And Ginny, too, for she soon made it abundantly obvious that she was much more than a magnificent body and a pretty face.

They ate in the marquee, leaving afterwards, to the unfeigned sorrow of everybody at the dig.

Then they took Ginny on a personally conducted tour of the Bay of Islands, the boys showing the place off with pride as they pointed out spots of interest.

'Fabulous names,' Ginny murmured. '*Urupukapuka*, superb! And *Waewaewetorea*. It's a beautiful language. Bourne, honey, you'll have to use some of these names in a song.'

Even this blatant endearment couldn't spoil Lorena's delight in the day, although Bourne's answer gave her some uneasiness.

'I've finished them,' he answered shortly, as if the subject bored him, then pointed out where a gannet dived into the water ahead of them.

As the hot sun drowsed down Gordon took them out to the Hole in the Wall at Piercy Island, although there was slightly too much swell for him to be confident enough to take the launch through. They saw the slim white pencil of the lighthouse on Cape Brett, no longer manned although the keepers' homes were still there, and made their way back into the dusk, calling at exquisite bays to show Ginny the best that the Bay could offer. At one of them Gordon cut the engine and they had dinner while the sun sank in a blaze of scarlet and the sky turned first green, then deep blue, finally losing all colour in the darkness as the stars beamed down.

The trip back was magic, for they sang and were silent and talked softly, and Bourne sat beside Lorena all of the way. And just before they arrived at the jetty he bent his head and kissed her, and she kissed him back, uncaring if anyone saw, refusing to admit to herself that she was content with whatever small crumbs he was prepared to offer her. Perhaps it was foolish, but she was sure that, whatever had happened in the past, he could no longer be Ginny's lover. He could not kiss one girl almost in front of his present mistress!

The next day was breathlessly hot, unpleasantly so. Lorena was co-opted by Mrs Haworth to help with the party, and spent the day in the homestead's big, efficient kitchen working like a galley-slave while one part of her mind wondered dismally what Bourne was doing.

Her confidence of the night before had evaporated like a morning mist, the kiss they had exchanged seemed a cheap gesture now. Ginny was so beautiful, so—*right* in every way, what hope had she? Perhaps Bourne had been just amusing himself.

But a tiny flame of hope kept itself alight in her breast, so that she prepared carefully for the dance, wearing her favourite summer outfit, a sun-frock which had been an extravagance one gloomy spring day. It had meant going without lunch for some time, but now, as she smoothed the frock over her hips, she was glad. The muted greens and apricots suited her tan to perfection, and her modest amount of make-up combined with excitement to give brilliance to her beauty.

When Bourne saw her he smiled in slow appreciation, letting his glance linger on the smooth comeliness of her arms and legs, the bare tanned expanse of her shoulders. Lorena felt extra colour mount high in her cheeks, but she returned his look with as cool a stare as she could, while her heart beat a rapid tattoo in her breast. He wore jeans and a thin shirt open at the neck to reveal the strong lines of his throat.

A cowboy, she thought, and then, no, a gypsy, for his eyes were challenging and bold, his dark sensuality overpowering. Anticipation lent a glitter of almost feverish intensity to Lorena's eyes; she turned away, afraid that she was revealing too much of the tension which had her in thrall.

So she missed Ginny's entrance, but not Bourne's reaction as the film star twirled in her full skirt and frilled blouse. He laughed into Ginny's knowing eyes, a husky note of provocation audible to Lorena's ears as if it was directed at her. And when Ginny stumbled—accidentally?—he caught her and held her for a long moment against him, his firm, cruel mouth enigmatically curved as he looked straight across her head at Lorena.

But Lorena would not let her spirits droop. She did not know what Bourne was up to, but she was not going to let him make a fool of her—ever again! So when they arrived at the woolshed and Mrs Howarth introduced her to a Peter somebody who had a most appreciative glint in his eyes she accepted his request to dance without hesitation.

The evening became an exercise in self-control. Everywhere she looked, it seemed, she saw Ginny and Bourne. Once, dancing with Gordon, she found herself wondering dismally if anyone else as heart-broken as she had ever danced in this woolshed. Self-pity was a contemptible emotion and she thrust it from her, forcing herself to be gay, to give pleasure even if she could no longer feel it.

'I think our woolshed affairs get better each year.' Gordon's voice was complacent, as if the function owed its success to him alone.

Lorena laughed. 'That's because you're now at an age when you enjoy them more,' she retorted. 'Still, you may be right. Everyone seems to be having a marvellous time.'

She said the same thing to Peter whoever-he-was during the next dance. He was young and eager and he very much wanted to make an impression, so she smiled and responded as if he had indeed done just that.

'*I'm* certainly having a marvellous time,' he told her meaningfully, his expression hopeful.

Almost imperceptibly Lorena moved away, a pang of guilt assailing her. She had no right to use him as a buffer against despair.

Unfortunately she caught a glimpse of Bourne again, dark head bent over Ginny, seemingly oblivious to anything but the effect she was having on him.

Hardening her heart, Lorena smiled deliberately into her partner's face, allowed him to draw her closer and began to act as if her very life depended on pretending that she was having a wonderful time. It gave her no pleasure to discover that Peter followed her lead with alacrity, grey eyes sparkling with excitement and anticipation as the evening wore on.

No doubt he thought he had discovered the ideal holiday romance. A strange, unnatural recklessness spurred Lorena on, so that she responded to his ever more audacious advances with none of the irritation such behaviour would normally rouse in her.

Like someone else, someone harder, someone looking for experience, she danced and flirted and talked, and when he steered her outside she went without a backward look, knowing what would be expected of her, careless of what would happen.

Defiantly she told herself that a little ordinary human warmth would be welcome after Bourne's behaviour, but when they reached the dimness of the trees which sheltered the sheepyards she felt a sick emptiness in her stomach, a shame which brought the blood rushing to her cheeks. She had thought Bourne's kiss cheap; what on earth could she call this behaviour?

But Peter did not deserve to be snubbed; he was merely following her lead. So when he kissed her she responded.

And he showed his essential niceness by saying softly, 'I've rushed you, haven't I?'

Miserably conscious of her own duplicity, she nodded into his shoulder.

'Don't worry,' he said gently. 'We've got all of the holidays yet. You're so beautiful, I can wait. Let's go back and dance.'

Which only increased her self-contempt, and the fury she felt at Bourne. It was stupid to blame him for her behaviour, but even more humiliating to know that just by ignoring her he could force her into a situation like this, so contrary to her principles that it might have been another girl who had slipped out from the woolshed.

The heavy rock beat of the record had ended while they were outside; through the open windows now came a slower, sweeter melody, a dance tune of Peggy and Sel's vintage. As they walked back Lorena stole a glance at her watch. Only eleven o'clock, which meant that there could be another three or four hours at least of this torment; on occasions the dance had ended with Mrs Haworth cooking a vast meal of bacon and eggs for everyone.

Lorena did not know how she could bear it.

And then they were inside, and Bourne took her hand, saying with crisp authority, 'Our dance, Lorena,' and she was swept away out on to the floor.

He said nothing, but she could feel the cruel strength of his fingers crushing hers, the hard pressure of his hand on her waist.

And when she lifted her eyes she met the darkness of his, ice-cold as the nethermost parts of hell.

'Your lipstick is smudged,' he said conversationally.

Lorena felt a cold chill of fear. Licking her lips, she could only respond inanely, 'Is it?'

'Yes. Enjoy yourself?'

But she would not permit him to question her as if she were a naughty child. With eyes fixed firmly on the opposite wall she said in as remote a voice as she could manage, 'Of course. Why?'

'I wondered. Care to come outside with me now?'

Her lashes lifted, met searing contempt. 'No,' she whispered, her precarious control cracking.

'Why? What has he got that I haven't? You've responded most satisfactorily to my kisses before. Don't tell me that you're only up for one man at a time; because I can prove that you're lying.'

White-faced but defiant, she snapped, 'Don't be

an idiot! You have no right to behave as if—as if I've done something awful!'

'Oh, come now,' he murmured, voice smooth as cream, 'attack might be the best form of defence, but it's not going to work this time.'

And he pulled her closer and laughed as she stiffened, tried to release herself.

'Listen, little flirt,' he said as he laid his cheek against hers, 'you picked the wrong man to try your tricks on. I don't care if people start wondering about exactly what's been happening between you and me; it won't worry me in the least if everyone thinks you're my mistress. And if you keep on pulling away I'm going to kiss you here and now.'

It was no idle threat. Lorena responded to the threat of determination in the deep slow tones by forcing herself to relax, unaware that her stormy eyes and flushed cheeks betrayed the turmoil within her.

'That's better, honey,' he said hatefully. 'Now, who's the boy-friend?'

'Peter.'

'Peter who?' She could not reply and he laughed. 'So you don't even know his other name! Fast workers, both of you. And to think that all this time I've held back because I thought you were still innocent!'

'Is that what it was?' she asked bitterly. 'Big of you.'

'Stupid of me.' Without missing a step he inclined his face, the skin of his cheek like rough silk against hers, and breathed into her ear, 'But I won't be so stupid again, I promise. If you want to be loved, Lorena, I've had a lot more experience than your new boy-friend. He looks a little callow; if you want to be pleasured as well as kissed, I'll show you how.'

Sickened to the core, she wrenched back, eyes a golden blaze beneath her delicate brows, her mouth wounded and trembling as she stood facing him. 'I don't want to be shown how,' she stated flatly, her voice hard with the control she was imposing on herself. 'Look, why don't you dance with Ginny? I'm quite sure she's missing you.'

Dancers swirled around them; even in her wrought state Lorena could see the curious stares of those who had to avoid them, but she no longer cared. The phrase 'moment of truth' had a hackneyed ring to it, but every instinct she possessed told her that for them this was indeed the moment of truth.

'She can look after herself,' he said indifferently, and beneath his breath, 'Come here, before I give you something to remember me by—for ever.'

'I don't care.'

But as she turned to plunge blindly towards the door he took her shoulder, turned her and held her hard against him, moving sensuously in time to the music.

A familiar languor sapped Lorena's defiance; on an indrawn breath she said painfully, 'Bourne—please . . .'

'Oh, shut up!' he snarled into her hair. 'God, but you sicken me! Little bitch, with your innocent eyes and soft, fresh mouth. I suppose you're as responsive as this with any man who touches you.'

His nearness stifled her, but she was not going to let him ride roughshod over her any longer.

'You've got the hide of a rhinoceros,' she said thickly. 'If I'm a flirt, what the hell are you?'

'Jealous?'

'No,' she lied. 'I *don't* care about you. I don't care who you sleep with. I don't care if I never see you again. Just leave me alone, will you! Make love to someone who appreciates it!'

He laughed at that, although there was danger in his laugh, in the uplift of his brows, in the crackling tension between them.

'You appreciate it,' he taunted. 'Too much, sweetheart. Don't worry—I'll leave, and you can do what you like.'

But Lorena stared up at him, her expression open and easily readable. For a long moment his handsome features stayed hard and predatory, then slowly they softened. 'I'm sorry,' he said unexpectedly. 'Don't think too hardly of me, my dear.'

'When are you going?' she whispered, caring no longer that she had probably revealed the secret she had tried so hard to hide.

'Tomorrow.'

And so he did, he and Ginny both. Apparently a telegram had arrived for him just before the dance to summon him back, and Ginny decided to go with him.

So they had a quiet Christmas after all, and after that another lot of guests arrived, fortunately more than enough to keep Lorena so busy that she could not spare the time during the day to think, and at night sheer exhaustion prevented too much introspection. She did not even weep much; her grief and loss went too deep for tears. But she was glad when it was time to leave Waiwhetu and go back to Auckland and the busy university year.

CHAPTER NINE

THE year passed like any other. There was the bustle of finding an apartment with Liz and another two girls, the inevitable small frictions as the roommates settled in, the familiar, inexorable procession of the academic year.

Oddly enough Lorena found that she could work just as well; indeed her only solace was her work. All her good resolutions about finding something of value in this love of hers had gone by the board as soon as Bourne left; she had been kept busy at Waiwhetu, but in Auckland there were no demanding guests to keep her on her feet, and she had time to think, time which she filled with a ferocious energy for work.

For after a week or so she had moved around like an automaton, lost in a miasma of misery so black that she was aware of her friends viewing her with some alarm. This forced her to snap out of it; she made the discovery that one can appear outwardly as normal as ever, though a canker of grief and loss ate away at all happiness. She even went out, but allowed no man to touch her, not even to hold hands. Bourne had spoiled her even for the solace of the warmth of physical contact, she thought bitterly, and wondered if she was doomed to spend the rest of her life longing for one man only. It was so unfair, to fall headlong into love, so wholeheartedly that it seemed doubtful if she could ever recover her heart again, with a man who thought of her, if he thought of her at all, as a holiday romance, a woman who passed the time away until someone more profitable came along.

And she despised herself for the eagerness with which she read the gossip columns in the hope that his name might be there. Once it was, but the meagre little snippet merely stated that he was working on his new record, a precious scrap of information for her hungry heart.

In May she worked at a local nursery, potting up plants for the winter rush, for Peggy had said there was nothing for her to do at Waiwhetu. She was pleased; it seemed impossible that she could ever have been happy there.

It was shortly after this that Liz came in from an evening lecture and tossed a magazine at her. 'Here, I found this in the bus. If you look at page 30 you might find something interesting.'

It was a review of Bourne's latest L.P. Thankful that Liz had gone into her bedroom to change, Lorena read it carefully, the colour draining from her face as the words unfolded before her incredulous eyes.

The reviewer was ecstatic. The best ever, he wrote, the best Kerwood, and perhaps the best of the decade by anyone. '*Bourne Kerwood has in these songs refined his craft so that every track is a masterpiece in itself—distinct, yet linked by a common thread of emotion which only Kerwood could attempt without sentimentality. I found it almost impossible to choose one I liked best. Perhaps the title track,* Woman of Chaldea, *and then I played the next track,* I loved the Stars, *and another* Girl from the Far Isles, *and found myself quite unable to choose. Whoever the summer girl of the dedication is, and rumour has it that Bourne has finally found a true love at last, she can be proud of being the inspiration of an L.P. such as this. Superb is the only word I can use to describe it.*

There was more, but Lorena did not read it, beyond a cursory look at the title of each song, a look which confirmed her fears. Yes, he had everything—the song titles were a run-through of the weeks he had spent at Waiwhetu.

Very slowly she put the magazine to one side, bent and touched her toes to bring colour back to her face, then almost ran into the drab, tiny kitchenette to put the kettle on.

'Intriguing songs, aren't they?' Liz's voice was carefully casual. 'I suppose *Chequer Board from the Past* was inspired by the dig. I remember he commented on the chessboard effect. How about *Midnight is the Time to Die*?'

Lorena explained that hurried rescue trip in the launch, recalling the details with a clarity which revealed how sharply the incident was etched on her memory. That had been before she realised the strength of her love, but of course, even then she had been fathoms deep, a captive of his moody attraction.

'I think the idea is quite intriguing,' Liz commented. 'A musical record of your holiday. Nice if you can manage it. Are you getting the record?'

Lorena put instant coffee into mugs, poured the boiling water over and added milk, seeking some semblance of normality with the everyday banality of the task.

'I suppose so,' she said after a pause. 'I have every other one of his. Here, have some coffee, you must be frozen.'

'Not now I'm inside.' Liz sipped the brew gratefully, her brows knitted. Then, with the air of one who has made a decision from which there is no turning back, she said, 'You know, Lorena, have you ever thought that perhaps he did care? That L.P. sounds like a love letter to me.'

'Am I so transparent?' Lorena asked bitterly.

'Not in the least, but I saw you together, and I saw the way he looked at you. I thought then—' she spread her hands—'I thought that he was definitely interested. And when you arrived back here all—well, buttoned up, as if afraid of letting any emotion out, I put two and two together.'

'He was interested,' Lorena said tiredly, leaning back in her chair, transparent eyelids lowered to hide the naked pain beneath. 'In an affair. And old-fashioned though it might be, that's not what I wanted.'

'Tough.' Liz was sympathetic, but not cloying. 'But how do you explain the songs? I mean—*Miss Independence*, and there's another one that the chap says is the best love song he's heard, *Clear as Glass, Tough as Steel*. And the one he praises so highly at the end, *You turned Away*.'

'All that it means is that like all creative artists he's able to use any material that comes his way as a base for his work.'

Liz wasn't convinced, but all she said was, 'Well, I'm going to listen to the record carefully.'

'Come on!' Lorena exclaimed. 'Liz, do you really think that Bourne Kerwood could possibly have any interest in me, other than the most basic?'

'Why not? Honestly, girl, anyone would think you were a real crab! You're intelligent, you've got the kind of integrity which is, as he puts it, clear as glass, tough as steel, and you're certainly not behind when it comes to figure or face. He's not a god, when all's said and done.'

Lorena smiled at Liz's vehemence, was warmed by it even as she rejected her words. 'You saw the competition,' she said drily, draining her coffee cup. 'And really, Liz, even if he had offered marriage, I doubt if I'd have accepted.'

'What?'

Lorena shrugged. 'You could hardly say that the track record for entertainers' marriages is particularly good. It would kill me if—well, it's not likely to happen. For me marriage is for ever.'

'I see your point.' But Liz didn't sound convinced, though she said no more about it, not then or in the days that followed.

Lorena buried herself in her work, while two tracks from the record climbed the hit parades and she couldn't turn the radio on without hearing Bourne's voice telling her that she was as clear as glass, as tough as steel, or alternatively asking the woman of Chaldea why she had left him.

Perhaps it was the winter she blamed it on, perhaps her unquiet heart aggravated by the fear of hearing the record for the first time, but she grew thin and pale. Then one night when the rain poured down and a cold southerly buffeted the city a friend brought the L.P. round. Lorena ignored Liz's swift, sympathetic glance; screwing her courage to the sticking point, she even put the thing on the turntable herself, but she was glad when Liz turned the main light out, even more grateful when Bourne's deep voice caressed her ears, velvety or raw with emotion, exciting as never before as he documented a love affair which had been doomed from the start.

When it was over they paid it the supreme accolade of silence, for a moment. Lorena fought desperately for control. Her every nerve was pierced with a desolation so intense that she thought for a moment she would be unable to move or speak without breaking down.

Then Liz said in a blessedly matter-of-fact voice, 'Well, who's for coffee? After that orgy of emotion I need something a little bitter.'

'I'll make it,' Lorena offered, on her feet before anyone else could rise, thankful of a chance to regain more of her composure before facing the others.

If they noticed that Lorena said very little in the subsequent discussion nobody mentioned it; possibly her reticence was accepted by now as an essential part of her character. And when they had gone Liz said nothing, apparently deciding that silence was more soothing than any words, however sympathetic, could be.

August passed, cold and wet, and then it was the rush of almost hysterical cramming for examinations. Only this year Lorena found it easy to cope with the tensions and worry; it was almost as though her life was divided into two mutually exclusive parts, the emotional plane where she ached for Bourne with a longing which time only intensified, and the ordinary everyday life where examinations had to be taken and papers presented, where it was quite easy to pretend to be her normal self.

Towards the end of the term she heard from Peggy and Sel. She would not be needed this Christmas as there were to be no visitors; Mr Read had given them their air fares to Australia and they planned to visit Sel's sister in Brisbane there. Apparently Bourne had told Mr Read how well they had looked after Waiwhetu, for his surprise gift was intended as a bonus for their efforts and care.

'So although we'll miss you it's too good an opportunity to miss,' Peggy wrote, 'as we've not seen Sel's sister for nearly twenty years. Have you decided what career you want to take up? Let us know when you're settled, won't you.'

'She sounds a bit casual!' Liz exclaimed when Lorena handed the page over. 'Still,' with a sharp glance at the sleek chestnut head, 'it's probably a good thing. You can set to and find yourself a proper job! Something that will set you on the road to a career.'

'I don't even know if I've got any qualifications,' Lorena protested half-heartedly.

'Oh, rubbish. You know jolly well you'll get your degree; you've worked like a slave all year and your term papers have been excellent. Have you any idea what to do?'

Lorena sighed, moved her chair so that she was in the patch of warm spring sunshine and poured herself a cup of tea before replying, 'No, I've no idea at all. When I came to 'varsity I thought I'd have three years to decide what to do, but I'm afraid they've been a waste of time as far as careers go. I have a great number of interests, but no burning ambition to do anything. So I'll just start at the beginning of the Sits. Vac. and start applying.'

'And if you find you hate what you're doing?'

She smiled. 'I'll chalk it up to experience and try again. After all, there must be *something* I'll find fulfilling. All I have to do is find it!'

Brave words, but after three weeks or so of trying

to find it Lorena began to wonder whether she was ever going to find a position which would take the place of her studies and fill up an existence which seemed to become more aimless every day. Until the arrival of Peggy's letter she had not realised just how much she had hoped for another summer at Waiwhetu; now, with that hope gone she found it extremely difficult to summon up the energy to keep going.

Already it seemed like summer. In every season the gardens of Auckland were gay with colour, but at this time there was an extra surge of light and gaiety in them, a warm fecundity in the earth which set the colours dancing and jingling against the greens of the foliage and the painted wooden houses. The harbour grew blue and glittering; the long strings of beaches became dotted with people catching the sun and refurbishing their water skills.

At night the air was soft and heavy and humid, and overhead the summer stars, bold Orion, the shy Pleiades and the cluster called the Hyades about the red eye of Taurus the Bull moved in majestic procession. But although Lorena attended the Observatory sessions she left her telescope in its case; the stars needed the brighter skies of Waiwhetu for her small telescope to see them properly.

Christmas drew close, forcing her to accept the fact that this year for the first time in her life she would be completely alone at Christmas. She did not look forward to it, but she was determined not to become too self-pitying. Meanwhile her search for a job went on with depressing results.

'It looks as though I'll have to go to business college and learn to type,' she told Liz cheerfully, and laughed at the other's horrified expression.

'There's no reason why not, you know. It would probably do me the world of good to learn something practical.'

'Why not, then?' Liz pulled her jacket into place. 'There, how do I look?'

'Very nice. I like that purply colour on you; it gives you a rich and opulent air. I hope your John appreciates it.'

A faint blush softened the severity of her friend's expression. 'He's not exactly my John yet, you know.'

'He soon will be. I've never seen a man so besotted.'

'Well, I hope so,' Liz returned candidly, 'because to be shamelessly honest, I'm rather besotted myself. To coin a phrase, I rather think that this is it.'

'Good. He's ideal for you.'

Liz hesitated, as though unsure of how her next remark would be taken, but made it anyway.

'I wish you could find someone as ideal for you. I hate to see you eating your heart out for someone who's unattainable.'

'Like a lovesick schoolgirl over a pop idol?' Lorena knew that her voice was too sharp; to cover up she smiled and went on wryly, 'Although I never went through that phase; perhaps it's just caught up with me a little late. And don't worry, Liz, unrequited love no longer causes girls to go into a decline and fade away. Nothing so ethereal; we liberated women are a much tougher lot to kill than our great-grandmothers.'

'You're right, of course.' But Liz sounded far from convinced. After a moment she added, 'Would you like to come home with me for Christmas? I wrote and asked Mum, heaven knows why, as our place is open house at any time of the year, and Mum says in her letter today that she'd love to have you.'

Lorena hesitated, met the other girl's clear gaze, and allowed her inclinations to coax her into accepting gratefully, for the idea of being alone at Christmas had begun to assume horrifying proportions in her mind. It didn't matter if Liz felt pity for her; they were close enough friends for such an emotion to be unimportant.

'Good! I'll write and tell her tomorrow.' Liz was clearly elated at Lorena's acquiescence, but wisely said nothing more on the subject.

John arrived almost immediately, then they were gone and Lorena was alone in the poky little apartment, still stuffy from the heat of the day, with no prospect of coolness until the sun set in an hour's time.

Restlessly she prowled the small room, feeling stifled by the walls, before deciding to go for a walk. About a mile down the street was a small park on the edge of one of Auckland's many hills with an outlook across to the harbour. A walk there would tire her a little, and communing with nature should give her some peace of heart.

Swiftly she pulled on a pair of lightweight slacks and a shirt, grimacing as she did so. All her clothes were old and tired-looking; anything new and fashionable would have to wait until she had several wage cheques in the bank.

A swift comb-through of her hair led to another grimace, and the decision to give her face some colour with lipstick. She had grown older, she was sure, by more than the year which had almost passed since Bourne had gone. Yet there was nothing to explain the increased maturity, no lines in the smooth skin, no drooping chin or mouth. Just a tiredness which dimmed the yellow-green of her eyes and a lack of sparkle which gave her an atmosphere of general dimness.

Head held high, she locked the door behind her, dropped the key into her bag and went down the steps, through the neglected garden and out on to the street.

The still air was warm, almost caressing her bare arms. Scents of flowers drifted across the pavement from the gardens on either side of the road; there were roses and bearded irises, the crimson torches of waratah trees, gladiolus-like spears in the soft air. Lorena decided, not for the first time, that glorious though gladioli and roses were in season if she had a garden she would grow them in the vegetable plot. They were so very stiffly formal, needing even more formal surroundings. Here they were at variance with the lush sub-tropical foliage, the skyline with its curious little volcanic cones, even with the seascape which was becoming visible between the houses on one side of the road.

Children rode up the quiet street on bicycles, calling to each other in their clear, high voices, laughing at nothing, teasing and pretending. Lorena remembered evenings like this in another suburb, not so far away, not so long ago as time went, and swallowed fiercely. Self-pity was a bore, and she had become enough of a bore already, wearing her heart on her sleeve. She would *not* give in to it!

Waiwhetu would be beautiful now, softly salt-scented, the garden a delicious dimness where the cat stalked invisible prey through the borders. If Peggy and Sel were still there they'd be walking around the garden in their usual companionable silence, Peggy stooping to pull a weed here and there, Sel's deep-set eyes noting work to be done on the morrow. And there would be the hush of the evening breeze in the pohutukawas, and the cry of the gulls as they wheeled overhead.

Lorena blew her nose.

A voice from behind drawled, 'Honey, if you're going to keep up that pace I'll need a rest every ten minutes.'

Incredulous, unable to believe her ears, she whirled around ... met laughter and mockery in his dark glance, and faltered *'Bourne!'*

'The very same guy.' His glance was watchful, his arm slipping naturally across her waist. 'Where are we going?'

'To the park.' Gesturing aimlessly down the street, she asked, 'How—where did you come from?'

'That car down the road. I asked the guy to drop me off behind you because I had a feeling you might refuse to get into a car with me.'

'Why?' she asked in stunned, flattened tones, still unable to believe that he wasn't an hallucination conjured up by her lonely heart.

He smiled at that, rather strangely. 'Well, we parted under somewhat difficult circumstances,' he returned enigmatically. 'Come on, show me the park.'

'What about the car?'

'He'll wait.'

Firmly he turned her, tucked his hand under her elbow and propelled her down the road, walking with the same noiseless tread which had so impressed her a year ago.

After the first delirious shock of joy Lorena felt caution flooding her emotions again, drowning out the happiness which his presence brought with a wave of antagonism. How dared he coax Peggy into giving him her address and then spy on her until he could get her where she couldn't avoid him? He had the nerve of a hippopotamus, she thought angrily, and if he thought she would be content to become his next light of love he had another think coming!

But she could not prevent herself from looking up once, it had to be at exactly the moment when he looked down at her, so that their glances caught and clung and it was Lorena who looked away, conscious that she had probably given herself away. Not that it mattered, she thought wearily; if he didn't know by now that she loved him he was by no means as experienced as she knew him to be.

'Here we are,' she said abruptly. 'If we go down this path we can see the harbour.'

The park was tiny, a patch of velvet lawn, a small clump of trees and a railed walk above the steep hill which had steps leading down to the road beneath. The path led through the dim shadows of the trees.

Lorena was not particularly surprised when Bourne stopped beneath a big oak, not startled when he lifted her chin and bent his head to kiss her. But the unleashed savagery of the embrace shocked her, as did her tumultuous response. Like a man who has returned to his wife after years away he made a soft groaning noise as he crushed her lips beneath his, not attempting to control the passion which sprang to life between them like a flower full-blown. And she—well, she clung to him unashamedly, moulding her body against the lean contours of his, her mouth tremulous and soft beneath his seeking lips, content for this moment to go on for ever.

But it could not, of course. Indeed, after that first tumultuous onslaught he put her from him, a strange smile pulling at the corners of his mouth, his expression almost calculating, partly mocking. Lorena sighed, knew that she would not be able to resist him when next he kissed her. If the absence had done nothing more it had revealed to her that her desire met and matched his and that her defences were far too easily overborne. If he wanted her he had only to say so; she seemed incapable of resisting.

'I've missed you,' he said casually, as if it had been only a few days since they had parted.

It was a stupid response, but she replied, 'I've missed you, too.'

'So I noticed.' Then swiftly, without giving her time to answer or even to think, 'Look, we have to talk. Do you want to walk back to your apartment, or will we take the car?'

'I don't mind,' she said unhelpfully, unable to think straight, unable even to make the proper responses. By arriving so unexpectedly he had stripped her of all her defences, no doubt according to plan, and she was incapable of coping, her senses caught up in the dangerous singing ecstasy of his presence.

He smiled at that, dropped a kiss on her cheek, careless of who saw them, and said in his deceptively slow drawl, 'O.K., we'll take the car. There'll be other times for walking.'

But once back inside the apartment, he seemed disinclined to talk. Instead he wandered around, touching things, flicking through the books while she made a cup of tea.

'We've run out of coffee,' she said, as she poured it.

He grimaced. 'Just as well, if it was instant. Thanks.' Then abruptly, 'Had a good year? Academically, I mean.'

'Yes.'

A narrow smile touched his lips. 'Do you think you've got your degree?'

'I think so,' she replied honestly, gazing into the clear amber depths of the tea.

'Good.' He drank, set his cup and saucer down with decision. 'I'd have been back for you earlier, only I thought you'd better get that degree. It's the sort of thing that nags, not graduating.'

With a detached interest Lorena noted that the surface of her tea was ruffled by tiny waves. Her hand was trembling. Without lifting her eyes she asked thinly, 'What exactly do you mean by that?'

'Exactly what I said.' He laughed, the mockery she had always disliked still there. 'Did you really think I was walking out on you for good, Lorena?'

The anger which was her only defence came to her aid now so that she put her cup down and looked directly at him, her pallor increasing, the green-amber of her glance very sparkling in the small shabby room.

'Yes, I did,' she said with spirit. 'Why should I not? You slammed out in a huff, arrogant, bad-tempered, with your mistress on your arm——'

'Point number one,' he interrupted blandly, eyes half-closed so that she couldn't read their expression. 'Ginny is not and was not then my mistress.'

'I don't believe you.'

'You'd better. She and I were lovers—oh, five, six years ago. Then we became friends. And don't curl your lip like that, you obstinate, cross-grained little fool. You liked her—admit it.'

'That's got nothing to do with——'

'Admit it,' he ordered relentlessly.

Lorena drew a breath, invigorated by his presence, aware now that even when she was arguing with him she was happier, more alive, than at any time in this year. 'Yes, I do like her,' she said reluctantly.

He grinned. 'Good. She likes you very much, partly because she thinks I've picked someone who's stopped me from being so damned cocksure, but also because of you yourself. You'll find her an absolutely loyal friend.'

But Lorena shook her head, summoning up the strength she knew she was going to need for the next few minutes. Better to get it over with, she thought bleakly, and even then wondered if she should seize what happiness he could give her, careless of the pain and disillusionment which could inevitably follow.

'What now?' he asked dangerously. 'Tell me, Lorena, why do you look as if I'm offering you a foretaste of hell? I know you love me; you must know now that I love you.'

Oh, but it was worse than she had ever dreamed pain could be. Feeling as if her heart was being torn from her breast, she got blindly to her feet, moving across to the window to stand with her back to him.

After a moment she began, 'I can't——', found that although the muscles of her throat worked no sound came forth and had to swallow convulsively before saying, 'Bourne, I'm not—I can't deny that I love you. But I'm not going to go with you.'

There was a moment's silence, then he was behind her, his fingers hard and hurtful on her arms as he turned her to face him, forced her to look up into an expression of such demonic ruthlessness that she quailed.

'Oh yes, you are,' he said softly, each word a threat. 'You're mine; you became my woman the first time I kissed you, and there was nothing you or I could do about it. I knew when I set eyes on you that you had the power to turn my world upside down with your serene mystery and the promise of your body, but I thought you would be engrossed with yourself like so many beautiful women. But you weren't, you aren't. You've got fire and courage and a temper that tops mine and a brain I like to explore, and you're *mine*. Body and soul, heart and mind!'

If he had kissed her then she knew that she would have become his in every way without delay, for her body responded with a surge of wanton desire which made her tremble with the effort to control it.

But he made no effort to touch her, beyond keeping his hands clasped tightly around her upper arms. He had gone oddly white under his tan and there was a smouldering ferocity in the depths of his eyes which warned her that his control was as sorely tried as hers.

White-lipped, she whispered, 'For how long, Bourne? A year—perhaps five? And then what? A well-publicised break-up?' With a fierceness which matched his she cried, 'I'd rather *die*! And

I'd see you dead before I'd let you go off with someone else.'

'It's more likely that I'll see you dead,' he retorted sombrely, his glance burning colour into her skin as it swept across her face and throat, lingered on the soft curve of her breast, then returned to the hollow in her throat where a little pulse beat rapidly, like the flutter of a butterfly's wing, beneath the pale silken texture of her skin. 'Oh—*God!*' he groaned, and bent, and touched his lips to that vulnerable hollow. 'Lorena, I can't wait any longer. Love me—even if you won't see me again. I've starved for you—spent nights walking the floor because I ached for you.'

His voice was thick as the rapid words tumbled over themselves, his mouth hot against her skin, his hands gentle yet shaking when he undid the buttons of her blouse. Lorena could not prevent him, betrayed by her own need and her compassion for a need she recognised as even greater than her own.

When he lifted her in his arms she drew his head down to hers and for the first time returned his kiss with no holding back, offering her mouth to his plundering search, her slender body resting against his with a languorous relaxation which was new to her.

'Darling,' she said huskily, against his lips, 'Bourne——'

His hand at her breast trembled, then he said violently, 'No!' and pushed her away from him so forcibly that she half fell on to the arm of the sofa.

Humiliation washed over her. Bottom teeth clenched on her lip as she began to pull the blouse around to cover herself. Bourne turned away, wiped sweat from his forehead and said tightly, 'I'm sorry. I didn't intend that to happen.'

'It's all right,' she said numbly; she found that she needed fierce concentration to guide the buttons into their holes and tuck the blouse into her slacks. It took her a ridiculous length of time to get tidy again. Fortunately her brain seemed to have lost its impetus somewhere so that she could not think sensibly. But she had been given a respite; later perhaps, she would be grateful for that.

'Lorena, I've obviously made a hash of everything,' he said quietly. 'Perhaps I'd better not look at you while I speak, because when I see you I can't think straight. Now, listen. I love you, and I want to marry you. I can't promise that we'll always stay married; I'm not sure enough of how you feel to do that, but I can swear to you that I'll never leave you. I think you've become part of me, so much a necessary part of my life that I'm only half a man without you.' He swung around, took her hands in a grip that crushed and continued rapidly, 'Now, will you please say "Yes, Bourne, I'd like to marry you" and then we'll go someplace so that I shan't seduce you, which is what I want to do more than anything else at the moment.'

But Lorena stared up into his face with such a bedazzled expression that he began to laugh, and then, before she knew it, she was laughing too, so that some of the tension evaporated and he pulled her into his arms and held her gently with tenderness, not passion, until she said softly, 'Of course I'll marry you, you idiot.'

After that it was a long time before either said anything sensible.

But at last, when the sunset had faded and the

moon was high in the soft summer sky he asked soberly, 'Does the idea of marrying me seem such a big step to take, honey?'

Lovingly she touched the corner of his mouth, her emotions transparent. 'Yes and no. I never dreamed you could love me, so I haven't even thought about marriage. But it's what I want more than anything in the world.'

'Good.' With common assent they had not indulged in passionate lovemaking; both knew that now that their love was spoken the physical revelation of it could wait. But he kissed the palm of her hand and closed her fingers over it, and his smile was mocking yet very tender. 'Because I live a very quiet life, you know. I don't go on the road much, and I intend giving that up before long. I have several homes scattered around, but they're all secluded. And I refuse to invite any but my closest friends to them. So if you want to see your name in the gossip columns you'll have to give up the idea. Your cruel husband has no intention of allowing it.'

Lorena's smile was warm, very loving, very radiant. 'I'm a private person myself, as you know.'

'As for marriages that end in divorce——' He put his finger on her pulse, feeling the surge of her life-force, through her veins. 'Well, there are plenty of them. What you don't hear about are the ones that last. And there are plenty of those, too. Part of the reason I stayed away so long was to give you time to find out for yourself exactly how you felt about me. I knew after the first week or so what I wanted from you, but I wanted an equal commitment from you. And you made it quite clear right at the start that you didn't want marriage—not then. So I had to be careful—make sure you were sure.'

'Is that why you were so nasty to me?' she asked, smiling. 'Warning me off? Or setting me tasks to overcome?'

He laughed and caught her against him, holding her very close so that she could smell the faint tang of aftershave, feel the hard strength of his muscles, the thunder of his heart against her cheek. 'No. I wanted you, and I had to have some method of stopping my lust from getting the better of my good intentions. I'm sorry I took off in such a hurry because I could see I was fighting a losing battle. The night of the dance I was so furious with you for flirting with that guy that I had to choose between punching his head in or punishing you.' His voice deepened, became muffled as he said into her hair, 'What I wanted to do was drag you into my bed and make love to you until you begged for mercy. I wanted to see you white and exhausted in my arms; put my mark on you so that it could never be effaced. But I knew that if I did that I'd lose whatever hope we had of a good marriage. So I did the next best thing.'

Unbearably shaken by the images his words aroused, Lorena said carefully, 'If you can call swearing at me as if I was a tramp and then stamping out of my life the next best thing!'

'Believe me, it was.' He sighed. 'I didn't think I had it in me to feel so murderous. When we love each other I want it to be perfect; I knew I'd spoil it all if I took you in anger, or before you knew what you really felt for me; I knew I wasn't going to last out much longer. You were so damned responsive—you seemed to melt into my arms! So I had to go.'

'I do love you,' she whispered. 'Oh, Bourne, I thought I'd die without ever being able to say that. When are we going to get married?'

'As soon as possible,' he said forcefully, tipping her face up to meet his glowing eyes. 'I'm full of good resolutions at the moment, but I don't know how long they'll last. Where would you like to go for a honeymoon?'

'I'll have to get a passport,' she said worriedly. 'Perhaps we'll have to honeymoon here.'

'Good, I'd like to see a little more of New Zealand. Can you drive?'

'Yes. Why?'

He laughed into her startled face. 'Because I drive on the right-hand side of the road, my darling. If anyone's going to drive on the left it will have to be you!'

But he learned quickly, and after a month of heaven it was he who drove her up to Waiwhetu, saying as the cattlestop rattled beneath the wheels, 'This is a beautiful country, darling, but I think this is the most beautiful spot in it.'

'My feeling exactly.' Lorena smiled at the gold band on her finger, thinking that happy though the day had been when he put it on her finger, the happiest day of her life was this one, each new one which found her waking beside him.

'So I'm glad Aaron Read has decided to sell it to us,' he said blandly, as if she had not spoken.

Slowly Lorena turned her head, saw the secret smile he was holding in check, felt her love expand within her.

'Truly, Bourne?'

'Truly.' He grinned, picked up her hand and held it beneath his on the wheel. 'I can be as sentimental as the next man, honey. We met here, so it's special. We'll come here as often as we can and be plain Mr and Mrs Kerwood, and Peg and Sel can look after it and get to know our children.'

Lorena felt that peculiar sensation in the pit of her stomach which only he could rouse. In a voice which was shaky and soft she said, 'It makes me feel odd to think of having your children.'

'Odd?' He stopped the car outside the garage, turned to look down at her, his expression broodingly tender. 'It makes me feel like shouting and singing and composing songs. It makes me feel like loving you until you cry for mercy. It makes me feel I'm the luckiest man in the world. Now, get out so that I can carry you across the threshold. We've had a lovely honeymoon, darling heart. This is where our life together starts.'

'With Peggy and Sel?' she asked demurely.

He laughed. 'No, they're still in Australia. We have a few days more to be alone in, but——' His voice deepened, became almost sombre in intensity. 'Sweetheart, however many other people there might be around us, you will always be the heart of my life. Just you.'

Lorena's breath stilled as she smiled at him. Like that, brooding, intent, his hands trembling slightly as they touched her eyelids and mouth, he was the lover who had initiated her into a world of the senses where passion blended with love and laughter.

'I do love you,' she said quietly. 'Just like I breathe—because I can't help myself. I think I must have loved you always, even before I met you.'

He laughed, and kissed her, his mouth tender yet tantalising. 'Of course. From the beginning to the end of time. Come on in, now. This is our time, and we mustn't waste it.'

He lifted her, carried her over the threshold and walked with her into the coolness of the house, so close that they did indeed seem to move as one person; joined by bands which they had forged in anger and resentment and love, which Lorena knew could only become stronger and more enduring as the years went by. She kissed him with a fervour which she revelled in showing, and went fearlessly with him towards their future.

HARLEQUIN SUPERROMANCE

Harlequin Reader Service

In U.S.A.
MPO Box 707
Niagara Falls, NY 14302

In Canada
649 Ontario St.
Stratford, Ont. N5A 6W2

Please send me the following HARLEQUIN SUPERROMANCES. I am enclosing my check or money order for $2.50 for each copy ordered, plus 59¢ to cover postage and handling.

- ☐ #1 END OF INNOCENCE
- ☐ #2 LOVE'S EMERALD FLAME
- ☐ #3 THE MUSIC OF PASSION
- ☐ #4 LOVE BEYOND DESIRE

Number of copies checked @ $2.50 each = ________
N.Y. and Ariz. residents add appropriate sales tax $________
Postage and handling $ .59
TOTAL $________

I enclose________.
(Please send check or money order. We cannot be responsible for cash sent through the mail.)
Prices subject to change without notice.

NAME________________________
(Please Print)
ADDRESS________________________
CITY________________________
STATE/PROV.________________________
ZIP/POSTAL CODE________________________

Offer expires Aug. 31, 1981

10156332341